THE WALLFLOWER'S UNSEEN CHARM

WALTZING WITH WALLFLOWERS (BOOK 1)

ROSE PEARSON

THE WALLFLOWER'S UNSEEN CHARM

PROLOGUE

"*Y*ou must promise me that you will *try*."

Miss Joy Bosworth rolled her eyes at her mother.

"Try to be more like my elder sisters, yes? That *is* what you mean, is it not?"

"And what is wrong with being like them?" Lady Halifax's stern tone told Joy in no uncertain terms that to criticize Bettina, Sarah, and Mary – all three of whom had married within the last few years – was a very poor decision indeed. Wincing, Joy fell silent and dropped her gaze to her lap as her beleaguered lady's maid continued to fix her hair. This was the third time that her lady's maid had set her hair, for the first two attempts had been deemed entirely unsuitable by Joy's mother – though quite what was wrong with it, Joy had been completely unable to see.

"You are much too forward, too quick to give your opinion," her mother continued, gazing at Joy's reflection in the looking glass, her eyes narrowing a little. "All of your elder sisters are quiet, though Bettina perhaps a little too much so, but their husbands greatly appreciate that about them!

They speak when they are asked to speak, give their opinion when it is desired and otherwise say very little when it comes to matters which do not concern them. *You,* on the other hand, speak when you are *not* asked to do so, give your opinion most readily, and say a great deal on *any* subject even when it does not concern you!"

Hearing the strong emphasis, Joy chose not to drop her head further, as her mother might have expected, but instead to lift her chin and look back steadily. She was not about to be cowed when it came to such a trait. In some ways, she was rather proud of her determination to speak as she thought, for she was the only one of her sisters who did so. Mayhap it was simply because she was the youngest, but Joy did not truly know why - she had always been deter-mined to speak up for herself and, simply because she was in London, was not, she thought, cause to alter herself now!

"You must find a suitable husband!" Exclaiming aloud, Lady Halifax threw up her hands, perhaps seeing the glint of steel in Joy's eyes. "Continuing to behave as you are will not attract anyone to you, I can assure you of that!"

"The *right* gentleman would still be attracted," Joy shot back, adding her own emphasis. "There must be some amongst society who do not feel the same way as you, Mother. I do not seek to disagree with you, only to suggest that there might be a little more consideration in some, or even a different viewpoint altogether!"

"I know what I am talking about!" Lady Halifax smote Joy gently on the shoulder though her expression was one of frustration. "I have already had three daughters wed and it would do you well to listen to me and my advice."

Joy did not know what to say. Yes, she had listened to her mother on many an occasion, but that did not mean that she had to take everything her mother said to heart... and on this occasion, she was certain that Lady Halifax was quite wrong.

"If I am not true to who I am, Mama, then will that not make for a very difficult marriage?"

"A difficult marriage?" This was said with such a degree of astonishment that Joy could not help but smile. "There is no such thing as a difficult marriage, not unless one of the two parties *within* the marriage itself attempts to make it so. Do you not understand, Joy? I am telling you to alter yourself so that you do *not* cause any difficulties, both for yourself now, and for your husband in the future."

The smile on Joy's face slipped and then blew away, her forehead furrowing as she looked at her mother again. Lady Halifax was everything a lady of quality ought to be, and she had trained each of her daughters to be as she was... except that Joy had never been the success her other daughters had been. Even now, the thought of stepping into marriage with a gentleman she barely knew, simply because he was deemed suitable, was rather horrifying to Joy, and was made all the worse by the idea that she would somehow have to pretend to be someone she was not!

"As I have said, Joy, you will try."

This time, Joy realized, it was not a question her mother had been asking her but a statement. A statement which said that she was expected to do nothing other than what her mother said – and to do so without question also.

I shall not lie.

"I think my hair is quite presentable now, Mama." Steadfastly refusing to either agree with or refuse what her mother had said, Joy sat up straight in her chair, her head lifting, her shoulders dropping low as she turned her head from side to side. "Very elegant, I must say."

"The ribbon is not the right color."

Joy resisted the urge to roll her eyes for what would be the second time.

"Mama, it is a light shade of green and it is threaded through the many braids Clara has tied my hair into. It is quite perfect and cannot be faulted. Besides, it does match the gown perfectly. You made certain of that yourself."

So saying, she threw a quick smile to her lady's maid and saw a twitch of Clara's lips before the maid bowed her head, stepping back so that Lady Halifax would not see the smile on her face.

"It is not quite as I would want it, but it will have to do." Lady Halifax sniffed and waved one hand in Clara's direction. "My daughter requires her gown now. And be quick about it, we are a little short on time."

"If you had not insisted that Clara do my hair on two further occasions, then we would not be in danger of being tardy," Joy remarked, rising from her chair, and walking across the room, quite missing the flash in her mother's eyes. "It was quite suitable the first time."

"*I* shall be the judge of that," came the sharp retort, as Lady Halifax stalked to the door. "Now do hurry up. The carriage is waiting, and I do not want us to bring the attention of the entire *ton* down upon us by walking in much later than any other!"

Joy sighed and nodded, turning back to where Clara was ready with her gown. Coming to London and seeking out a suitable match was not something she could get the least bit excited about, and this ball, rather than being a momentous one, filled with hope and expectation, felt like a heaviness on her shoulders. The sooner it was over, Joy considered, the happier she would be.

CHAPTER ONE

"*A*nd Lord Granger is seated there."

"Mm-hm."

Nudging Joy lightly, her mother scowled.

"You are not paying the least bit of attention! Instead, you are much too inclined towards staring! Though quite what you are staring at, I cannot imagine!"

Joy tilted her head but did not take her eyes away from what she had been looking at.

"I was wondering whether that lady there – the one with the rather ornate hairstyle – found it difficult to wear such a thing without difficulty or pain." The lady in question had what appeared to be a bird's nest of some description, adorned with feathers and lace, planted on one side of her head, with her hair going through it as though it were a part of the creation. There was also a bird sitting on the edge of the nest, though to Joy's eyes, it looked rather monstrous and not at all as it ought. "Surely it must be stuck to her head in some way." She could not keep a giggle back when the lady curtsied and then rose, only for her magnificent headpiece to wobble terribly. "Oh dear, perhaps it is not as well secured as it ought to be!"

"Will you stop speaking so loudly?"

The hiss from Lady Halifax had Joy's attention snapping back to her mother, a slight flush touching the edge of her cheeks as she realized that one or two of the other ladies near them were glancing in her direction. She had spoken a little too loudly for both her own good and her mother's liking.

"My apologies, Mama."

"I should think so!" Lady Halifax grabbed Joy's arm in a somewhat tight grip and then began to walk in the opposite direction of that taken by the lady with the magnificent hair. "Pray do not embarrass both me and yourself, with your hasty tongue!"

"I do not mean to," Joy muttered, allowing her mother to take her in whatever direction she wished. "I simply speak as I think."

"A trait I ought to have worked out of you by now, but instead, it seems determined to cling to you!" With a sigh, Lady Halifax shook her head. "Now look, do you see there?"

Coming to a hasty stop, Joy looked across the room, following the direction of her mother's gaze. "What is it that you wish me to look at, Mama?"

"Those young ladies there," came the reply. "Do you see them? They stand clustered together, hidden in the shadows of the ballroom. Even their own mothers or sponsors have given up on them!"

A frown tugged at Joy's forehead.

"I do not know what you are speaking of Mama."

"The wallflowers!" Lady Halifax turned sharply to Joy, her eyes flashing. "Do you not see them? They stand there, doing nothing other than adorning the wall. They are passed over constantly, ignored by the gentlemen of the *ton,* who care very little for their company."

"Then that is the fault of the gentlemen of the *ton,*" Joy answered, a little upset by her mother's remarks. "I do not think it is right to blame the young ladies for such a thing."

Lady Halifax groaned aloud, closing her eyes.

"Why do you willfully misunderstand? They are not wallflowers by choice, but because they are deemed as unsuitable for marriage, for one reason or another."

"Which, again, might not be their own doing."

"Perhaps, but all the same," Lady Halifax continued, sounding more exasperated than ever, "I have shown you these young ladies as a warning."

Joy's eyebrows shot towards her hairline.

"A warning?"

"Yes, that you will yourself become one such young lady if you do not begin to behave yourself and act as you ought." Moving so that she faced Joy directly, Lady Halifax narrowed her eyes a little. "You will find yourself standing there with them, doing nothing other than watching the gentlemen of London take various *other* young ladies out to dance, rather than showing any genuine interest in you. Would that not be painful? Would that not trouble you?"

The answer her mother wished her to give was evident to Joy, but she could not bring herself to say it. It was not that she wanted to cause her mother any pain, but that she could not permit herself to be false, not even if it would bring her a little comfort.

"It might," she admitted, eventually, as Lady Halifax let out another stifled groan, clearly exasperated. "But as I have said before, Mama, I do not wish to be courted by a gentleman who is unaware of my true nature. I do not see why I should hide myself away, simply so that I can please a suitor. If such a thing were to happen, if I were to be willing to act in that way, it would not make for a happy arrangement. Sooner or later, my real self would return to the fore, and then what would my husband do? It is not as though he could step back from our marriage. Therefore, I would be condemning both him and myself, to a life of misery. I do not think that would be at all agreeable."

"That is where you are wrong." Lady Halifax lifted her chin, though she looked straight ahead. "To be wed is the most satisfactory situation one can find oneself in, regardless of the circumstances. It is not as though you will spend a great deal of time with your husband so, therefore, you will never need to reveal your 'true nature', as you put it."

The more her mother talked, the more Joy found herself growing almost despondent, such was the picture Lady Halifax was painting of what would be waiting for her. She understood that yes, she was here to find a suitable match, but to then remove to her husband's estate, where she would spend most of her days alone and only be in her husband's company whenever he desired it, did not seem to Joy to be a very pleasant circumstance. That would be very dull indeed, would it not? Her existence would become small, insignificant, and utterly banal, and that was certainly *not* the future Joy wanted for herself.

"Now, do lift your head up, stand tall, and smile," came the command. "We must go and speak to Lord Falconer and Lord Dartford at once."

Joy hid her sigh by lowering her head, her eyes squeezing closed for a few moments. There was no time to protest, however, no time to explain to her mother that what had just been discussed had settled Joy's mind against such things as this, for Lady Halifax once more marched Joy across the room and, before she knew it, introduced Joy to the two gentlemen whom she had pointed out, as well as to one Lady Dartford, who was Lord Dartford's mother.

"Good evening." Joy rose from her curtsey and tried to smile, though her smile was a little lackluster. "How very glad I am to make your acquaintance."

"Said quite perfectly." Lord Dartford chuckled, his dark eyes sweeping across her features, then dropping down to her frame as Joy blushed furiously. "So, you are next in line to try your hand at the marriage mart?"

"Next in line?"

"Yes." Lord Dartford waved a hand as though to dismiss her words and her irritation, which Joy had attempted to make more than evident by the sweep of her eyebrow. "You have three elder sisters do you not?"

"Yes, I do." Joy kept her eyebrows lifted. "All of whom are all now wed and settled."

"And now you must do the same." Lord Dartford chuckled, but Joy did not smile. The sound was not a pleasant one. "Unfortunately, none of your sisters were able to catch my eye and, alas, I do not think that you will be able to do so either."

"Dartford!"

His mother's gasp of horror was clear, but Joy merely smiled, her stomach twisting at the sheer arrogance which the gentleman had displayed.

"That is a little forward of you, Lord Dartford," she remarked, speaking quite clearly, and ignoring the way that her mother set one hand to the small of her back in clear warning. "What is to say that I would have any interest in *your* company?"

This response wiped the smile from Lord Dartford's face. His dark eyes narrowed, and his jaw set but, much to

Joy's delight, his friend began to guffaw, slapping Lord Dartford on the shoulder.

"You have certainly been set in your place!" Lord Falconer laughed as Joy looked back into Lord Dartford's angry expression without flinching. "And the lady is quite right, that was one of the most superior things I have heard you say this evening!"

"Only this evening?" Enjoying herself far too much, Joy tilted her head and let a smile dance across her features. "Again, Lord Dartford, I ask you what difference it would make to me to have a gentleman such as yourself interested in furthering their acquaintance with me? It is not as though I must simply accept every gentleman who comes to seek me out, is it? And I can assure you, I certainly would not accept you!"

Lord Falconer laughed again but Lord Dartford's eyes narrowed all the more, his jaw tight and his frame stiff with clear anger and frustration.

"I do not think a young lady such as yourself should display such audacity, Miss Bosworth."

"And if I want your opinion, Lord Dartford, then I will ask you for it," Joy shot back, just as quickly. "Thus far, I do not recall doing so."

"We must excuse ourselves."

The hand that had been on Joy's back now turned into a pressing force that propelled her away from Lord Dartford, Lord Falconer, and Lady Dartford – the latter of whom was standing, staring at Joy with wide eyes, her face a little pale.

"Do excuse us."

Lady Halifax inclined her head and then took Joy's hand, grasping it tightly rather than with any gentleness whatsoever, dragging her away from the gentlemen she had only just introduced Joy to.

"Mama, you are hurting me!" Pulling her hand away, Joy scowled when her mother rounded on her. "Please, you must stop–"

"Do you know what you have done?"

The hissed words from her mother had Joy stopping short, a little surprised at her mother's vehemence.

"I have done nothing other than speak my mind and set Lord Dartford – someone who purports to be a gentleman – back into his place. I do not know what makes him think that I would have *any* interest in–"

"News of this will spread through London!" Lady Halifax blinked furiously, and it was only then that Joy saw the tears in her mother's eyes. "This is your very first ball on the eve of your come out, and you decide to speak with such force and impudence to the Earl of Dartford?"

A writhing began to roll itself around Joy's stomach.

"I do not know what you mean. I did nothing wrong."

"It is not about wrong or right," came the reply, as Lady Halifax whispered with force towards Joy. "It is about wisdom. You did not speak with any wisdom this evening, and now news of what you did will spread throughout society. Lady Dartford will see to that."

Joy lifted her shoulders and then let them fall.

"I could not permit Lord Dartford to speak to me in such a way. I am worthy of respect, am I not?"

"You could have ignored him!" Lady Halifax threw up her hands, no longer managing to maintain her composure, garnering the attention of one or two others nearby. "You did not have to say a single thing! A simple look – or a slight curl of the lip – would have sufficed. Instead, you did precisely what I told you not to do and now news of your audacity will spread through London. Lady Dartford is one of the most prolific gossips in all of London and given that you insulted her son, I fear for what she will say."

Joy kept her chin lifted.

"Mama, Lady Dartford was shocked at her own son's remarks to me."

"But that does not mean that she will speak of *him* in the same way that she will speak of you," Lady Halifax told her, a single tear falling as red spots appeared on her cheeks. "Do you not understand, Joy?"

"Lord Falconer laughed at what I said."

Lady Halifax closed her eyes.

"That means nothing, other than the fact that he found your remarks and your behavior to be mirthful. It will not save your reputation."

"I did nothing to ruin my reputation."

"Oh, but you did." A flash came into her mother's eyes. "You may not see it as yet, but I can assure you, you have done yourself a great deal of damage. I warned you, I *asked* you to be cautious and instead, you did the opposite. Now, within the first ball of the Season, your sharp tongue and your determination to speak as you please has brought you into greater difficulty than you can imagine." Her eyes closed, a heavy sigh breaking from her. "Mayhap you will become a wallflower after all."

CHAPTER TWO

"*D*id you hear what she said to Lord Dartford?"

Henry yawned and sat back in his chair, letting his gaze rove around Whites.

"I do not think I care a great deal as to who said what and to whom."

"Whyever not?" Lord Falconer sat down heavily, a glass in his hand. "It was more than a little delightful, I can assure you!"

Henry sighed and closed his eyes.

"I have no interest in it all, I am afraid. I care not as to whether Lord Dartford was insulted and while I certainly am delighted with this young lady's response to his arrogance, I do not particularly care who she is or what has become of her."

Lord Falconer sighed.

"Very well, though I think that very dull of you."

With a shrug, Henry fell silent, allowing his thoughts to settle. He had not been in London for long but his intention this Season was to find a young lady to whom he might give the title of 'wife'. She had to have particular traits within her character, of course, for he required someone who knew precisely what was to be asked of them and nothing more. Whether or not he would find that particular young lady here this Season, Henry could not say. If he had to return in the autumn, or for the following Season, then that was what he would do. This was much too serious a situation for him to simply pick any young lady based on how pretty she was.

"What is it that you are thinking of?" Lord Falconer nudged Henry, who let out a low groan. "Come now, you cannot be sitting there without having anything in your mind. What is it?"

"Nothing of any importance." Barely throwing his friend a glance, Henry picked up his brandy and took a sip. "Did you enjoy the evening?"

"Yes, immensely." Lord Falconer smiled broadly. "Though I am not here to find a suitable young lady or any such thing as that. I am simply here to enjoy myself this Season."

Henry shifted in his chair so that he might study Lord Falconer a little more closely. "You mean to say that you are simply here for the enjoyment of the Season? Nothing more?" Lord Falconer nodded enthusiastically. "And you care nothing for making a match?"

A loud guffaw broke through the quietness of White's and Henry winced, sitting forward in his chair just as Lord Falconer slapped him on the shoulder.

"Why should I care about such things? I am young enough not to require a wife as yet."

"But your heir?"

Lord Falconer shrugged.

"I have a younger brother who has a family of his own. Should anything happen to me, then he would take on the title. I have very little concern as regards that."

"Whereas I have no one save for myself." With a slight scowl, Henry picked up his brandy again. "I have no mother, no father, no brother or even sister!"

"You are quite alone in the world."

Henry's scowl grew. That was said without any sort of emotional understanding whatsoever, as though whatever Henry had just said did not bring even a flicker of sympathy to Lord Falconer's heart. It was rather difficult at times to be so alone, to have no family other than himself and a vague, distant relation or two – though most of them lived in Scotland, and he did not get to be in their company very often at all.

"Alas, you must have a much more pressing need than I to find a bride," Lord Falconer continued, a grin spreading across his face. "Should you like me to aid you in your search?"

"No, indeed not!" The scowl immediately broke apart as Henry grinned at his friend, aware that Lord Falconer's interest in young ladies of the *ton* was based solely on their appearance, rather than on anything of their quality of character. "But I thank you for your concern."

"One thing I should say, however, is that the young lady who spoke to Lord Dartford in such a way ought to be avoided, if you are looking for a young lady to marry. I do not think that she would suit you at all well."

His interest now a little piqued, Henry turned to face his friend.

"You say she spoke to Lord Dartford about his arrogance?"

"She did." Lord Falconer chuckled, shaking his head. "I could not quite believe what she said and the strength with which she said it, but it came from her lips without hesitation!"

Henry grimaced.

"I certainly should *not* desire a young lady who speaks without thinking, nor one who speaks to the gentlemen of the *ton* with anything akin to an improper boldness."

Lord Falconer grinned.

"Lord Dartford did deserve her cut, however. His arrogance is unmatched through all of London!"

"All the same," Henry countered, "I should have preferred her to remain silent and to have ignored him, for surely that would have been more fitting."

"Mayhap, but it certainly would not have been as entertaining!"

Laughing, Henry shook his head and then finished his brandy, getting to his feet thereafter.

"I think I shall need to return home. It is getting late, and I do not want to be tardy tomorrow."

"Tomorrow?"

Henry nodded.

"I am to call on Lady Eltringham and her daughter, Lady Judith. She and I are related, you know. Second cousins, I believe."

"Oh." Lord Falconer's eyes flared. "Lady Judith?"

"Yes." Dragging the word out, Henry narrowed his eyes at his friend. "Why? You have something to say about her?"

"No, not in the least, especially if she is your cousin." From the grin that Lord Falconer was desperately trying to hide, Henry did not believe a single word of his declaration, his stomach twisting with sudden, sharp nerves. "I do hope that you enjoy your visit tomorrow."

"I thank you – though, as I have said, she is my second cousin, which is really nothing at all." Realizing that it was no good to push his friend to tell him whatever was on his mind, Henry kept his gaze fixed on him, but Lord Falconer only continued to grin. "I think it will go well. Lady Judith seemed to be a very quiet, respectable sort."

"You do not know her?"

"No, as I have said, we are only second cousins, and I was not introduced to her until recently."

A gleam came into Lord Falconer's eye.

"Indeed? Then let us hope that your expectations are fulfilled."

"Let us hope so." Making to leave, Henry was stopped by Lord Falconer's voice calling him back. Swinging back around, he let out an exasperated sigh. "Yes?"

"I have one thing to ask," Lord Falconer said, still smiling. "When you have finished your visit to Lady Judith, come to my house and tell me all about it."

Henry opened his mouth to ask what it was that Lord Falconer knew, which he did not, but seeing his friend lift his glass to his mouth, his eyebrows arching, realized that there was nothing he could do to convince him to speak honestly. With a scowl and a nod, he turned on his heel and walked out of White's.

"Did you hear about that young lady who spoke so rudely to Lord Dartford?"

Henry sighed inwardly but forced a smile to his lips.

"Yes, Lady Eltringham, I did. I did think that–"

"We were speaking about it together, were we not?"

"Yes, Mama, we were." Lady Judith clicked her tongue and then leaned a little further forward, catching Henry's full attention. "Did you know that she told Lord Dartford that she would not be interested in him and his attentions, even if he should offer them to her?"

Henry blinked.

"I... I do not see how such a statement is in any way improper. In fact, I–"

"Do you not?" Lady Judith sat back in her chair, turning to face her mother again. "Did you hear that, Mama? Lord Yarmouth does not think there is any difficulty in a young lady speaking her mind so."

A frown drew itself across Henry's forehead as he looked from one to the other. The moment he had sat down in the chair in Lord and Lady Eltringham's drawing room, Lady Judith had begun to speak – and thus far, both she and her mother had not stopped talking. There had barely been any opportunity for him to talk and, whenever he did so, it was a struggle to finish his sentence.

Evidently, Lady Judith was not as quiet a soul as he had anticipated.

"I think that most strange, Lord Yarmouth." Lady Eltringham shook her head. "I have always taught my daughter to keep her thoughts to herself as much as she can. I should not *dream* of ever insisting that she speak all of her thoughts aloud!"

This was something of a peculiar statement given that thus far, Lady Judith had spoken about everything and anything she had wished, never once giving herself pause. Henry sat silently, looking from mother to daughter and realizing now that his first impressions of Lady Judith had been utterly mistaken. Yes, she was his cousin, but he did not know her, and now was quite sure that he had no desire to further his connection with her, either.

"The gentleman was arrogant, certainly, but everyone *knows* that he is so," Lady Judith continued, quickly. "There was no need to embarrass him in such a way by throwing his words back at him!"

Henry's frown became deeper.

"You mean to say that *he* was the one who first stated that he would have no interest in this young lady? That he was the one–"

"He said that to Miss Bosworth, yes." Lady Judith nodded as her mother murmured the same. "That is exactly what was said."

"And then Miss Bosworth told Lord Dartford that *she* would have no interest in his company either and, even though they have both said the very same thing, Lord Dartford is the one who is pitied, and this Miss Bosworth held up as an example of how a young lady ought *not* to behave?"

It was the first time during his visit that he had been able to speak for so long without being interrupted and, satisfied with himself, Henry picked up his tea and took a sip of the lukewarm, pale liquid, though he did not much like the taste. Silence settled across the room, with Lady Eltringham and her daughter sharing a long glance that told Henry very little.

He had no idea what they were thinking, be it either what he had said, or of he himself, but at this juncture, he did not particularly mind. The fact that Lady Judith had turned out to be an entirely different character from what he had expected told him that his expectations for this afternoon's visit were certainly *not* going to be met. He would not wish to call upon her again, nor take her out for a carriage ride, or the like. This visit would be more than enough.

"I confess that I am a little surprised to hear a gentleman speak in such a way." Lady Eltringham sniffed and arched an eyebrow in her daughter's direction. "I would have thought that propriety would have been expected in all things."

"Indeed it is, for both gentlemen *and* ladies," Henry agreed, quickly. "I do not think it fair to hold this young lady – Miss Bosworth, did you say? – to account, whilst leaving Lord Dartford entirely without blame. To my ears, it sounds as though he was being rather rude in his manner." The silence which followed told Henry that his time for this visit had come to an end and, with a smile, he rose to his feet and inclined his head. "Thank you both for the tea and the cakes. I have enjoyed my visit."

The two ladies rose as one, with Lady Eltringham gesturing to her daughter.

"And will you call again, Lord Yarmouth? We are kin, after all! I know my daughter would be glad to see you."

Henry cleared his throat, shuffling his feet a little as he clasped his hands behind his back.

"I am certain that we shall be in company together again soon, Lady Eltringham. Lady Judith, good afternoon."

It was neither a promise that he would return, nor an outright refusal, and Henry hurried from the room, glad to be finished with the visit. Making his way to his carriage, he stepped inside, only to jump with surprise when he discovered that none other than Lord Falconer sat there also.

"I was passing by and saw your carriage," he said, as Henry rapped on the roof, eager to take his leave. "I hope that you do not mind me waiting for you?"

"You do not have your own carriage?" Henry narrowed his eyes a little. "And this is a strange place to simply be passing by." When his friend grinned, Henry could not help but snort with laughter. "You came here deliberately, did you not?"

"I did." Lord Falconer chuckled, his eyes twinkling. "I could not wait to see just how you fared with Lady Judith. She is not as you expected her to be, I think?"

"She certainly is not!" Henry rolled his eyes. "I do wish you had told me earlier."

"What good would it have done? You would have still had to call."

"But I would have been more prepared and less disappointed."

Lord Falconer shrugged, the smile still on his face.

"But then I would have been less amused. To see your expression as you came out of the house was *most* entertaining." Laughing, he slapped his knee as Henry broke into laughter along with his friend, unable to help himself. "What did you speak of? Or were you unable to speak, given all that Lady Judith and her mother said?"

"It was difficult to speak a single sentence without being interrupted!" Henry sighed heavily and looked out of the window. "They *also* spoke of Miss Bosworth and Lord Dartford, though I found myself a little more intrigued than when you spoke to me of it."

"Oh?"

Henry nodded.

"It seems unfair that the lady should be considered at fault when she did the very same as Lord Dartford. He said he did not think that he would be at all interested in encouraging their acquaintance and she said the same, did she not?"

Lord Falconer's expression changed from laughter to consideration, his smile slipping and his brows knotting together.

"Yes, I suppose that is so."

"And yet society blames her for speaking bluntly. I do not think that fair." A quiet laugh broke through his words, making Lord Falconer frown in confusion. "I confess that, in saying such things to these two ladies, it was the only time that I found myself able to speak at any length, and without interruption! Once I had finished speaking, they both fell silent for some time!"

"Goodness, you must have shocked them!" Lord Falconer chuckled and grinned a little ruefully. "It does seem a pity that they would also be speaking poorly of Miss Bosworth, however, given what you have said. I had not thought of it before, but now I can see your point of view."

Henry shrugged.

"There is nothing to be done, I suppose. I do hope that the young lady is not too upset by the whole affair." Sighing, he leaned his head back against the squabs. "Regardless, I think that I am quite ready to attend another ball and be introduced to new acquaintances... though mayhap I ought to be a good deal more considered than before!"

"Do not let your first impression of a lady give you heavy expectations of her true character, yes," Lord Falconer agreed, firmly. "And make sure to stay away from Lady Judith unless you wish to have even the *smallest* conversation without interruption!"

Henry laughed and agreed wholeheartedly though, as his carriage continued to drive him home, he found his thoughts lingering on the unfortunate Miss Bosworth, wondering whether he would have the opportunity to meet *her* at the next ball, or if society's harsh judgments would have already pushed her far away from them all.

CHAPTER THREE

"*I* did warn you."

Joy closed her eyes and heaved a sigh.

"Mama, I do not need you to express your chagrin."

"No, what you *needed* was to listen to me! Had you done so, then you might not be standing at the back of the ballroom with very few others around you!" Lady Halifax clicked her tongue, clearly a little distressed over the situation while, at the same time, obviously blaming Joy for what had taken place. "You might have had gentlemen calling on you! You might have had your dance card filled entirely! But instead, you have nothing other than the shadows to accompany you."

Joy scowled and folded her arms across her chest. For the last sennight, the *ton* had come alive with rumors and whispers... and most of them had been about her, and what she had said to Lord Dartford. Lady Dartford had done as Lady Halifax had expected and, within the week, Joy was now considered to be uncouth, blunt, and much too forward for any young lady... though with the latter sentiment, Joy could not help but agree with.

"We can try again," her mother suggested, heaving a long sigh. "Here, take my arm and we shall walk around the ballroom again."

"And have every gentleman snort with laughter as he turns his head away, and every lady whisper about me to her friend? I do not think I shall do so."

"But what else are we to do?" With what sounded like a wail, Lady Halifax threw up her hands and then closed her eyes. "I am meant to find you a suitable gentleman to wed and instead, I am standing with you at the very back of the ballroom with no hope of *ever* doing so."

Joy let her hands fall to her sides. Initially, she had laughed off the concerns her mother had expressed, whereas now, she was beginning to feel a little ashamed of how boldly she had brushed off her words and how unconcerned she had been. Yes, she wanted to be as she truly was, yes, she wanted to speak as she felt, but she had never wanted *this* situation. Her mother was clearly despairing, lost, and adrift, given that she did not have a purpose any longer. Try as she might to help Joy integrate into society, she was going to fail, simply because of Joy's unwillingness to listen and act upon her mother's advice.

"I think we simply need a little time, Mama," she said, finding nothing else to suggest. "Did you not always tell me – and my sisters – that society has nothing better to do than to whisper about others? And that these whispers will always fade into something else in time?"

Lady Halifax nodded, but her expression was somewhat forlorn, breaking Joy's heart. She was the reason for her mother's upset, and the only hope she could offer her at present was that, in time, things might change.

"Why do you not go and speak to some of your friends,

Mama?" she asked, hoping that it might encourage her mother a little. "I can stay here."

Shaking her head, Lady Halifax let out another long breath.

"It would not be right. You could..."

"You can see that no one here is going to trouble me," Joy interjected as her mother's sentences ran off into nothing. "I will stay here, and you can go to speak with your friends for a short while. That will bring you a little happiness, yes?"

Lady Halifax frowned.

"I suppose it would bring me a little contentment, yes. Are you sure that you will be quite all right?"

Joy nodded and watched as Lady Halifax walked away without even a backward glance, leaving Joy quite alone. Seeing that she was in the shadows and that no one was even looking at her, Joy let herself slump back against the wall, no longer standing as tall and as upright as she ought to be. Her heart grew heavy as she watched the dancing couples step out for the quadrille, her stomach twisting as regret burned a path up into her chest. Why had she been so determined not to listen to her mother's warnings? And what was to become of her now?

"You are Miss Bosworth, are you not?"

A little surprised, Joy started and turned, seeing a young lady with dark eyes looking at her, a small smile on her face.

"Yes, yes I am." Pushing herself up to stand properly, Joy frowned. "Are we acquainted?"

"No, but I hope it will not be long until we are friends," came the reply. "I am Miss Emma Fairley. There is also Miss Rachel Simmons, Lady Alice, and Lady Frederica." Twisting her head, she gestured to the small group clustered nearby, whom Joy had not noticed before this moment. "For various reasons, we are all forced to stand at the back of events such as these, watching rather than taking part."

"Then you are all wallflowers?"

The lady did not take insult, as Joy might have expected, but instead, Miss Fairley simply nodded.

"And you come to speak with me because... you think I am a wallflower also?"

"Are you not?"

Joy opened her mouth to say in no uncertain terms that she certainly was *not* a wallflower, only for her to keep such words back. Was she not just as Miss Fairley had said? Was she not a wallflower?

I suppose that I am.

"You would be welcome to join us," Miss Fairley continued, entirely unaware of Joy's inner thoughts. "It can be a lonely circumstance to stand here by oneself."

She did not wait for Joy to agree or disagree, but rather simply walked back to the other ladies, leaving it up to Joy as to whether or not she would go with her. Perhaps, Joy considered, Miss Fairley knew what it was like when one was first pushed to the edge of society. It took a good deal of consideration and acceptance, for the difficulties being a wallflower presented were very difficult to take in.

"But that is what I am now," she murmured to herself, turning her head away from the other ladies. "I have no gentlemen seeking me out. I have no acquaintances eager to be in my company. So what else is there for me?"

With a sigh, she turned to face the other ladies and, after a few minutes, made her way to them. Four smiling faces met her and, though she was not in the mood to smile – why would she be, after being demoted to being nothing other than a wallflower – Joy did her best to return them.

"Allow me to make the introductions," Miss Fairley said

quickly, gesturing to each lady in turn as she spoke. Joy did her best to listen carefully to each name, nodding and smiling at each one though her stomach still roiled with a mixture of confusion, upset, and mortification.

"And this is Miss Joy Bosworth," Miss Fairley finished, making Joy realize that she had never once introduced herself to the lady. Miss Fairley knew precisely who she was, even without the introductions, though Joy did not ever recall being introduced. Evidently, her face was already recognizable by even the wallflowers of society.

Her embarrassment burned all the hotter.

"You will find yourself amongst friends here," Miss Simmons murmured, perhaps seeing the uncertainty on Joy's face. "No one will judge you, you can be assured of that."

"Indeed." Lady Alice smiled, and Joy nodded back at her, not certain what to say. "I am the daughter of an Earl and yet still you find me standing here, hiding myself away."

"Though that is not your fault," came a quick reply from Miss Fairley.

"But apparently, *I* am being ignored by society simply because I am a little too outspoken." Joy suddenly found her voice, her expression growing darker as she flung one hand out towards the rest of the room as though to blame each and every person standing there. "Though I do not think I can justify being overly upset, given that my mother warned me not to behave in such a way."

Lady Frederica stepped forward and grasped Joy's hand in a quick expression of solidarity.

"My dear lady, you are certainly *not* to be blamed for such a thing. I heard that Lord Dartford was very rude indeed, and spoke to you in a manner which deserved such a response from you!"

Joy managed a wry smile, appreciating the support from the lady.

"Mayhap. I confess that I am not certain any longer."

"What did he say to you?" Lady Frederica's eyes sharpened. "Was it as I have heard?"

Nodding, Joy recalled the conversation in perfect clarity.

"First, he asked if he was correct in stating that I had elder sisters and when I said he was correct, his response was, 'Unfortunately none of your sisters were able to catch my eye and, alas, I do not think that you will be able to do so either'."

There was a collective gasp and Joy let her lips curve ruefully.

"That is dreadful. How could he think to say such a thing?" Lady Alice took a step closer to Joy, her eyes searching Joy's face. "And your response to him was that you did not think that a concern, given that you would not be drawn to him either."

"It was something akin to that, certainly, though said with a good deal of emphasis." Slowly, Joy's embarrassment faded to nothing, a kinship beginning to soften her heart and a slow growing sense of understanding settling her upset. "But now what is there for me to do, but stand here, alongside all of you, and wait until society decides to forgive me for my supposed mistake."

There came a few nods, and one sorrowful sigh, though Lady Frederica – who had released Joy's hand – shook her head firmly.

"No, I do not agree. We continue to do our best and to stand in amongst society whenever we have the opportunity. I will not permit myself to be pushed away, to be squashed by the weight of whatever society wishes to throw upon me. I think that deeply unfair and I, for one, am determined to stand against it."

A faint flurry of hope ran through Joy's heart.

"I should like to do so too, but, given that my very reason for being placed in this position in the first place has been my own hasty speech and blunt manner, I am not certain of what I should, or ought to do."

Lady Frederica smiled.

"You will find opportunity and when it comes, you must grasp it with both hands."

"And do not let this circumstance alter you in any way," Miss Simmons said, coming to stand beside Lady Frederica. "You say that you speak bluntly and with too much haste and, were that a true difficulty, one which caused a good many problems then yes, I would encourage you to curb such behavior as best you could. But given what I have heard, it does not seem as though that is a great concern. Instead, it appears that society has treated you unfairly, while allowing Lord Dartford to do as he pleases! Therefore, I would not attempt to do anything to alter yourself, for there is no need."

"Not unless you wish to find a husband," Lady Alice interjected quietly. "That is what we are all here for, is it not? We all wish to find happiness."

Joy, looking from one face to another, took a long breath, and then let it out slowly, thinking through what had been said before she spoke – something which she did not do very often.

"I have already told my mother that I want to marry a gentleman who knows me as I am, not someone who thinks I am a quiet mouse of a lady who does not dare open her mouth unless someone has spoken to her. Lady Halifax, my mother, insists that I need to be so to even attract the attention of a gentleman and I confess, after this incident, I have begun to wonder if she is right."

Lady Alice smiled gently.

"I do not wish to insult your mother, but in this situation, I think it is wrong to tell you not to be who you are. To hide your character for, not only this moment but potentially for the rest of your life, would not bring you any sort of happiness. No, Miss Bosworth, if you can, then remain just as you are and know that you have friends here who will support you with that."

"Thank you." Joy took a breath, smiling as she released it, feeling a good deal better than she had done in some days. "I am certain that I will come to value your support a great deal." Looking around the group, her heart lifted a little and her smile grew. "How glad I am to have been able to find friends here. It is going to make the situation a good deal more tolerable, at least!"

The ladies all smiled their agreement and Joy turned back to look out at the ballroom again. If society did not like her as she was, then she would stand here with the other wallflowers but quietly refuse to change who she was to appease the *ton*.

Whether she would find a suitable match, however, Joy did not know. Considering this, her smile faded quickly. Would she be left standing here until the Season came to an end? Or was there even the smallest hope that *someone* might allow her to catch their attention?

CHAPTER FOUR

*H*enry looked around the ballroom, a faint smile on his lips. Surely there had to be some young ladies here who might be of interest to him?

"You are smiling to yourself again." Lord Falconer nudged him. "What is it that you are thinking of?"

"Whether one of these young ladies might become my bride." When Lord Falconer snorted, Henry shot him a hard look. "You may laugh, but I am quite serious about my determination to marry this year. It is my duty."

"And mine also, but I am not as eager as you to find the most perfect, the most correct young lady," came the reply. "I believe that should someone be of interest to me, they will come into my sphere and I will take notice of them. I do not have to go searching, nor do I have to be as considered in my thinking as regards the young ladies of the *ton*."

Henry sniffed and shook his head in disagreement.

"I am very different from you in that regard. I will not merely wait in the hope that someone comes into my sphere, as you say, but rather I must search for them and make certain that they are the most suitable of young ladies for me." He shot his friend a wry smile. "After my experience with Lady Judith, I realize now how cautious I must be!"

Lord Falconer chuckled.

"All the same, you need not be *too* careful. What if someone unexpected makes themselves known to you? What shall you do then?"

With a grin, Henry shook his head.

"I hardly think that will happen. All the young ladies of the *ton* are very similar in most ways. It is not as though any of them *can* be unexpected!"

Screwing up his expression, Lord Falconer opened his mouth to speak, only for his eyes to catch on something which he had not previously noticed, his eyes sharpening a little.

"Yes, I am wearing my late father's talisman," Henry said, seeing Lord Falconer's expression and speaking before Lord Falconer could remark on it.

"Why are you wearing it?" Lord Falconer tilted his head, his eyes still upon it. "It is not like you to do so. Usually, you only wear your own signet ring."

Henry shrugged.

"I wanted to do so. Seeking out a bride is more than a little significant, and wearing my father's gold talisman ring brings the situation a little more significance – at least to my mind."

Lord Falconer chuckled suddenly.

"And it is pure gold, with one very precious diamond and, therefore, very expensive which must, in turn, make young ladies aware of your wealth and standing, yes?"

A hint of embarrassment began to burn its way up Henry's chest and into his face, though he only cleared his throat and shrugged. His friend had hit upon the truth, but

Henry did not want to admit it. It seemed a little shallow to say that the only reason he was wearing what was a very expensive ring was simply to bring attention to his wealth but, all the same, that *was* the main reason for him doing so.

"Very well, I shall not tease you about it any longer," Lord Falconer chuckled, slapping Henry on the shoulder. "Come now, let us go and speak with some young ladies, rather than standing here, speaking *about* them."

"Only make sure to take a turn to your left rather than to your right." Henry nudged his friend lightly, tilting his head to the right. "Your cousin, Lady Judith, and her mother are standing over there and I am doing my best to avoid them."

Lord Falconer laughed aloud and, grinning, Henry walked alongside his friend in the opposite direction from the two ladies, his heart filled with expectation and anticipation of all the evening was to bring.

"IT BELONGED TO MY LATE FATHER." Henry held out his hand for Miss Blakefield to see, only to then quickly slide the ring off his finger and hand it to her. "I have subsequently had my own signet ring made, but my father's talisman, I keep with me also."

"I can see why you would do so!" Miss Blakefield smiled brightly, then dropped her gaze to the ring again. "It is quite beautiful... and heavier than I would have expected a ring to be."

Henry wanted to tell her that it was made of pure gold but refrained. There was no need to labor the point, no need to go into detail about how valuable this was. Instead, he allowed the lady's gaze to linger on it before taking it back from her, a light smile on his face.

"I thank you. You have a keen eye, Miss Blakefield, to see such a thing!"

"How could I not notice it?" she asked, glancing at her mother who had turned away a little, making the conversation between Henry and herself a little more private. "It is a beautiful thing, and it must be very precious indeed to have something linked to your beloved father."

Nodding, Henry slipped the ring back onto his little finger.

"That is very true, Miss Blakefield. He was an excellent man and I miss his presence and his advice a great deal."

"But *you* are the Viscount now," she said, making Henry frown. "That is important too. It does seem to be a great pity that we must lose the ones we love to gain such standing for ourselves."

Blinking, Henry took a few moments before he replied. Did she mean to be as callous as she had sounded?

"Yes, that is true, I suppose."

"Though I am sure there must be a little gladness when news of one's father's passing comes."

"Gladness?" It was as if a cold hand gripped at Henry's heart as he looked into Miss Blakefield's eyes, wondering at her meaning. "Why should one be glad at the death of one's parent?"

"Because," she smiled, her eyes bright as though she had very little awareness of the pain she was causing him, "there is the acknowledgment then that *you* now hold the title, that *you* have the fortune and the social standing that once belonged to your father. There must be some happiness in that, I am sure."

The grip around Henry's heart pulled tighter and he

cleared his throat gruffly, suddenly wishing he had not shown Miss Blakefield the talisman.

"Perhaps, Miss Blakefield, though I did not feel one iota of gladness."

"Oh." She frowned as though he were the one confusing her, rather than the other way around. "That seems a little strange." Her smile grew quickly as she shrugged. "However, I suppose such things do not matter. You are the Viscount now and, as such, have the title and all that comes with it. You will be looking to produce an heir very soon, I should think."

The shock of her words hit Henry so hard that he took a step back.

"I – yes. Do excuse me, Miss Blakefield, I hear that the waltz has been called and I must go to find the lady I am to dance with. Pray forgive me."

Miss Blakefield's smile froze and her eyes flared.

"But you have not signed *my* dance card, Lord Yarmouth!" she exclaimed, though Henry merely bowed and hurried away, making his way through the crowd, and doing his utmost to stay clear of both Miss Blakefield and Lady Judith. Closing his eyes, he let out a heavy sigh and shook his head, pinching the bridge of his nose.

"Are you dancing the waltz, Lord Yarmouth?" Just as he was thinking that very thought, none other than Lady Judith waved her dance card at him, hurrying towards him as though she were steeped in darkness and he was the only one carrying the light. "Cousin?"

"I – I am already engaged for the waltz, Lady Judith," Henry called, moving quickly away. "Forgive me!"

And now I must find someone to dance with.

He could not be seen hiding away in the shadows, not after what he had just said by way of excuse to Miss Blakefield *and* Lady Judith but, who exactly was he to dance with now? Turning his head, he looked all around him, only to spy a young lady standing by the wall, her arms folded and a sharpness about her expression. No one was with her, no parents, no chaperone or the like, and thus he ought not to approach, only for his breath to catch as the music began.

"Will you dance with me?" It was most unorthodox to walk towards a young lady in this manner and practically beg for her to stand up with him, but what else was there for him to do? He *had* to dance the waltz and yet he did not know this young lady and had never been introduced to her. "Unless, for some reason, you ought not to dance?"

The lady lifted her chin.

"There is no reason I ought not to dance."

"And are you permitted to dance the waltz?" Glancing over his shoulder, Henry snatched in a breath as Miss Blakefield and her mother came into view, having come wandering after him, perhaps to make certain that he *was* doing as he had said. "Please, might we step out together?"

"You do not know me." The young lady came closer to him, her eyes flashing as she looked into his face. "We have not been introduced."

"Then permit me to do so now. I am Viscount Yarmouth." Bowing, he offered her his arm. "And you would be doing me a great favor."

The lady hesitated, her eyes going over his shoulder only for them to flash back to his face.

"You are being pursued, I think."

Henry turned, groaning aloud when not only Miss Blakefield caught his eye but, thereafter, Lady Judith who was still waving the dance card in her hand.

"Yes, I am."

"And you are unwilling to be caught," she said, a light

smile on her face, bringing his attention to her green eyes which sparked with laughter. "Very well, Lord Yarmouth, let us step out together – though I warn you, you may find yourself the subject of conversation for dancing with a wallflower."

"That is quite all right."

When she put her hand on his arm, Henry let out a slow breath of relief and stepped forward, hurrying the lady through the crowd of dancers so that they might melt into the center, hidden from view by the many other gentlemen and ladies who were dancing also. He was not a moment too soon, for the music began as they reached the center and thus, Henry had to step forward and catch the lady in his arms without so much as a bow.

"I thank you," he murmured, beginning to turn gently, making sure not to knock into any other dancers. "This has saved me a great deal of strife."

The lady looked back at him, her feet moving in careful steps, never once going awry.

"The young lady in question was quite hopeful that I would dance with her," Henry continued, feeling as though he was required to give her an explanation for his haste. "I had the desire to step away, however, and made an excuse."

"You lied." The lady lifted an eyebrow and Henry took his gaze from hers, heat in his chest. She put it so bluntly, so clearly, that it was not something he could argue against.

"Yes, I suppose I did."

"You should have told her the truth," she said, quietly. "You ought to have told her that you did not want to dance and then take your leave. Otherwise, she would not have been pursuing you, and you would not have had to pull a wallflower out to dance the waltz with you."

Henry waited for a sense of frustration to build within

him, for his irritation to grow into something more but, instead, all that came was a quiet acceptance that yes, she was quite right. He ought *not* to have lied to Miss Blakefield, for now look at what he had been forced to do. There was nothing wrong with dancing with a wallflower – indeed, she was an exceptional dancer – but he had only done so because he had been attempting to hide from Miss Blakefield. Had he been honest, then she would not have questioned, for even a moment, where he was and what he was doing.

"Was she very disagreeable?"

The softness in the young lady's voice made Henry glance back into her eyes, letting his gaze take her in as he thought about the question. There was a gentleness to the vivid green of her eyes, and her red curls bounced gently as they waltzed. Why did he find himself eager to tell her all?

"I am afraid that Miss Blakefield was a little more insulting than she might have realized," he found himself saying, without having made a clear decision in his mind to tell this young lady the truth. "She spoke of how there was a gladness within the heart of a gentleman upon gaining the title."

The young lady frowned, her eyes still fixed to his.

"Gladness upon receiving the title?" she repeated as Henry continued to spin them around the room, her words coming in short bursts as the dance continued. "To think there would be joy in learning of the death of one's parent is utterly preposterous!"

Henry smiled then, relief spreading out across his chest.

"Yes, that is precisely what I thought. I knew then that there could be no further connection between myself and the lady."

With a brief smile that faded as soon as it had shown

itself, the lady turned her head a little and let the dance continue. Henry said nothing more, concentrating on his steps, but finding himself glad that the young lady agreed with him, even though he had not thought himself in need of such reassurance.

When the dance came to a close a few minutes later, Henry was surprised at how much he did not want it to end. Keeping hold of the young lady's hand, he bowed over it, then smiled into her eyes.

"I thank you."

"Of course." Taking her hand away quickly, she dropped into a curtsey. "I will make my way back in amongst the crowd of dancers before it is noticed that you have danced with me. I should not like to give you any more difficulty."

Henry wanted to ask her what she meant, his hand going out to hers again but, before a single word could be uttered, she had smiled, turned, and walked away from him, pulling herself into the crowd of gentlemen and ladies as they all walked from the dance floor, so that she was barely noticeable, not even by Henry himself.

And I did not ask her what her name was.

Shame bit down hard and Henry groaned aloud, rubbing one hand over his eyes as he realized how foolish he had been. With a sigh, he walked in the same direction he had seen her go, but she was nowhere to be found. Thinking that he might hurry back to the same place where he had first met her, he was suddenly accosted by Lord Falconer who, with a grin, slapped Henry on the back.

"Was it Miss Blakefield you danced with, old boy? I thought you might rub along very well with her."

Henry scowled, his eyes still on the edge of the ballroom as he looked for the young lady.

"No, it was not. I chose to step away from her rather quickly once she told me that I must have had some happiness on the day that my father died."

Lord Falconer's expression changed at once, his eyes flaring wide.

"I beg your pardon?"

"Indeed," Henry sighed, his shoulders dropping as he realized that the young lady in question was as good as lost. "I could not quite believe it and, when she told me that all that mattered was title, standing, and fortune, I knew that there was nothing more to be said between us. I took myself from her by making an excuse and was then forced to ask a young lady to step out with me – and no, before you ask, I do not know who she was for I did not ask her name."

Lord Falconer's eyes rounded.

"That is most unlike you."

"Be that as it may, I had no other choice," Henry returned, quickly. "I perhaps ought not to have lied but I chose to do so and then was forced to waltz with a stranger."

"And you do not know who she was?"

Henry shook his head.

"No, I do not." Another heavy breath tore from him, and he dropped his head. "I do not have the same anticipation as I did before. Thus far, I have tried to avoid Lady Judith and thereafter, ended up making a connection with Miss Blakefield, only to then desire to remove myself from her just as quickly!"

"Do not give up hope," Lord Falconer said, firmly. "Take a look around the ballroom and see just how many young ladies are present."

"And just how many of them would be suitable? How many would offer me what I require?"

Lord Falconer shrugged.

"I suppose it depends on how particular you are determined to be."

Henry sighed and shook his head, looking away from his friend and finding himself wondering about the young lady he had stood up to dance with. Could there be a chance that she might be the one lady he found more delightful than any other? Or was it foolish for him to even think about such a thing?

CHAPTER FIVE

"*A*nother ball."

Sighing, Joy leaned back against the wall, her head resting against it as she let her gaze rove quite freely through the ballroom.

"Indeed, Miss Fairley, though this time, at least I am not standing alone and wondering what is to become of me!"

Her new friend smiled.

"That is true, I think – though I did hear Lady Alice speaking with you about dancing?" Her head tilted, her eyes filled with questions. "Did you dance recently?"

Joy nodded, her smile growing as she recalled the strange incident which had seen her waltzing with a handsome – and clearly concerned – gentleman.

"Yes, Lord Yarmouth asked me to dance with him. Or, what I should say, is that he begged me to dance with him and I could not refuse."

Miss Fairley's eyes widened.

"Good gracious, whatever happened?"

Briefly, Joy told her what had taken place, laughing when she saw her friend's eyes grow even wider than they were already. She had known that it had been a very strange circumstance but clearly, it had been made all the more unlikely given that she was a wallflower.

"Though no one appears to have noticed that it was I who was dancing with the gentleman," Joy finished, with a small, somewhat sad smile as her shoulders dropped just a little. "Even my own mother did not notice."

Miss Fairley's lips pursed, and she shook her head.

"It is the difficulty with being a wallflower, I think. We are not taken notice of and since our names are not well known within society, it is easy enough to ignore us on the rare occasions when we *do* step out."

"And the gentleman did not ask my name," Joy added, as Miss Fairley clicked her tongue. "Clearly I was only present to solve his problem, and he did not need to know much about me at all, save for the fact that I would be willing to dance with him without the proper introductions."

Miss Fairley smiled softly.

"It must have been wonderful to dance the waltz, however. Did you enjoy it?"

Joy considered this, remembering how she had felt being swept into the gentleman's arms, spinning around and around the dance floor with him. Lord Yarmouth had been eager to converse and, though the situation had been a little overwhelming, she had found herself delighting in every moment. The way he had held her hand so tightly, the other at her waist as his green eyes had held her gaze certainly ignited some excitement within her heart, but that had soon faded once she had stepped out of his arms again.

"It was enjoyable, yes," she admitted, quietly, "but it was over much too quickly. I suppose it will not be repeated again soon either."

Miss Fairley sighed gently and looked out across the room. From where she stood, Joy saw the hope shining in her eyes and, with a sudden resolve, turned and gripped Miss Fairley's hand.

"I do not think that I am satisfied with being a wallflower."

Her friend blinked, her eyes rounding in surprise.

"Nor am I, but what can be done?"

"We must do *something*," Joy stated, with more emphasis than she had used before. "Listen to me, all of you." Turning, she waved one hand, garnering the attention of the other wallflowers. "Here we are, all standing here at the back of the ballroom without hope of stepping out to dance, without the expectation of good company or the like – and for what reason? None of us have done anything worthy of condemnation. We have been pushed aside by society, but that does not mean that we have to remain as we are."

Lady Alice frowned.

"I do not understand what you mean. We are wallflowers. What more can we expect?"

"We do not have to do as society expects of us," Joy said, emphatically. "They state that wallflowers must stand at the back of the room, silent and unimposing. I say that we do *not* have to do as they demand. Instead, we might walk, two or three together, about the ballroom, in amongst the guests, and seek to be seen and to be noticed. It might not change a great deal about our situation, but it will make us feel more significant, will it not? It will make certain that we are not forgotten! Even if society thinks we ought not to do anything akin to such a thing, why should it matter? We are already wallflowers. Do we truly wish to act as they demand? Do we wish to shrink back, to hide ourselves away and sink back into the darkness?"

The other ladies looked at one another, though Lady Alice had begun to nod, and a smile was forming across Miss Simmons' face.

"We could stand together and converse as so many others do." Coming a little closer, Miss Simmons' voice filled with excitement. "We do not have to hide here, do we? We could stand in amongst the other guests and talk together if no one else wishes to talk to us. What could be wrong with that?"

"There is *nothing* wrong with that," Joy stated, firmly. "It will take courage, certainly, but I, for one, am quite determined to step out and behave just as I please. Society might continue to call me a wallflower, but I will not behave as one."

There were a few murmurs as the ladies looked at one another and Joy held her breath, aware that her forward manner and determination might not be as any of the other wallflowers had expected. Some of them, having already been pushed into this position by society, could be a little too afraid to do anything of the sort, whereas others, such as Lady Alice, were eager to return to society in whatever way they could.

"I do not know what my mother would think." Miss Simmons' lips pursed, her gaze a little unsteady. "I fear what she would think."

"My own mother might also have something to say on the matter," Joy acknowledged, her heart a little heavy as she glanced around her, realizing that her mother had stepped away from her again. This was becoming a more regular occurrence and seemed to happen to almost every wallflower. "Though she is not here and might not even see me walk about the ballroom – but even if she did, then what of it? I am not alone, I am not without company. There can be nothing said against that in terms of propriety."

Miss Simmons nodded slowly, though she did not immediately appear enthusiastic. "That is true."

"My father would be most displeased." Lady Frederica bit her lip, her eyes downcast. "Though I confess I have had the same determination as you, Miss Bosworth, but as yet have been unable to find the courage to do such a thing."

"Then let us do so together." Joy held out her arm and, with a lift of her eyes and a smile, Lady Frederica came closer and took it, slipping her arm through Joy's. "Would anyone else wish to join us?"

Lady Alice nodded and stepped forward, linking arms on Joy's other side. Looking at Miss Simmons and Miss Fairley, Joy smiled in what she hoped was an encouraging manner but said nothing, not wishing to push them to do as they were.

"Be strong," Miss Simmons murmured, lifting her chin, and speaking half to herself before stepping forward. "Yes, I will join you and attempt to do all that I can to force society to see me, despite what they think of me and my standing."

"As will I... though perhaps you and I should walk together, Miss Simmons? I think that if we all link arms, we will cause a great deal of mayhem and then what will become of us?"

Joy laughed, a sudden, fresh hope filling her, lifting her heart and making her smile.

"Perhaps mayhem is exactly what society needs from us!" she exclaimed, as her friends laughed along with her. "Come then, let us walk around the ballroom slowly, looking at everyone without shrinking back. Stand tall, walk with strength and determination, and show the *ton* that we will not allow them to push us back into the shadows!"

～

"Well, this is more... intimidating than I had expected."

Joy nodded but did not allow the light smile to pull from her features.

"Everyone is looking at us, yes, but what is that to us? It is simply a look, nothing more."

Lady Alice drew in a long breath and nodded, coming to a stop, and then turning to face Joy.

"Mayhap we can stop here and speak together, though what we are to speak about I do not know!"

Her eyes darted left and right but Lady Frederica quickly caught her hand and squeezed it, reassuring the lady.

"Let us speak of the weather," she said, with a quiet laugh, "or mayhap where our favorite walks are. We may feel ill at ease, may feel uncertain and confused, but we need not let those around us see such things. If society is to get used to our presence here, we must also become used to being out amongst the gentlemen and ladies of the *ton*."

"I think you are quite correct," Joy agreed, quickly. "Lady Alice, which do you prefer, Hyde Park or St James' Park?"

While Lady Alice answered, Joy let her gaze rove gently, taking in the various faces near her and wondering what each of them thought, seeing three wallflowers standing amongst them, talking together. Inwardly, she tried to shrug off her concerns, though her heart was beating a little more quickly than usual. The sidelong glances and gloved hands lifting to hide whispers were not easy to ignore.

A sudden flash caught her eye and, frowning, Joy caught sight of a small, gold ring sitting on the floor only a short distance away. It was soon hidden from her sight as the other guests moved around but, excusing herself, she hurried across the room and, despite being aware that others would notice her behavior, bent to pick it up. Without even stopping to look at it, she turned back to her friends and joined them quickly, noting their curious glances.

"I saw something." Opening her hand, she frowned over the gold ring, noting the diamond placed within it and the crest which was engraved into the center. "This was on the floor."

"Goodness! Your eyes must have been very keen to see such a thing." Lady Alice wrinkled her nose as she studied it. "I do not recognize the crest, but then again, I do not have a vast knowledge of such things."

"Nor I, though I would say that this is an expensive item," Lady Frederica murmured, taking the ring from Joy's hand and examining it carefully. "What will you do with it?"

It was only when Lady Frederica held it between her thumb and finger that a sudden familiarity with the ring rose in her mind. Her eyes flared, her heart thudding in her chest as she stared at the ring.

I have seen that before.

It took her a few minutes to realize where she had seen the ring before, but once it came to her, a broad smile spread across her face, and she plucked the ring gently back from Lady Frederica.

"I know who this belongs to." Triumphant, she grinned

at Lady Alice and Lady Frederica. "It belongs to the gentleman who danced with me only two days ago."

Lady Alice's eyes widened.

"Does it? Are you certain?"

"Quite certain," Joy said, clasping the ring tight into her hand again. "I noticed it when he took my hand in his. That ring belongs to none other than Lord Yarmouth."

CHAPTER SIX

*H*enry yawned widely, stretched his legs out, and crossed them at the ankle. The ball had been very busy indeed and he had felt himself eager to retire from it a little early. Thus, he had come to White's and was now very comfortable indeed, sipping some fine French brandy and enjoying every moment of the quiet that surrounded him.

It did not last for quite as long as he had hoped for, given that the door opened and three gentlemen stumbled in together, with one of them being none other than Lord Falconer.

"Yarmouth! You left the ball much too early!" Seeing him, his friend came over at once, sitting down opposite as the other two gentlemen joined them, though they had not been invited. "You are acquainted with Lord Knoxbridge and Lord Mallory, I think?"

Henry nodded, acknowledging them both with a look.

"The ball was a little overcrowded for my liking."

"And you found yourself somewhat disappointed that the young lady you have been searching for, the one who fulfills all that you require, did not make herself known to you?"

Seeing the grin on his friend's face, Henry accepted the light-hearted comment in good grace, shrugging and waving to the footman to bring them all a glass of brandy.

"I met one or two young ladies whom I intend to call upon."

"Oh?" Lord Knoxbridge lifted his eyebrows. "Might I enquire as to who they were?"

"Why?" Henry tilted his head. "Are you seeking a bride also?"

Lord Knoxbridge nodded, no hint of a smile on his face, and Henry smiled, relieved that he was not about to be mocked for his intentions. Lord Falconer was doing quite enough of that.

"I was introduced to Lady Isabella," he said, frowning as he recalled how overbearing her mother had been, "and to a Miss Hereford."

Nodding, Lord Knoxbridge took the glass from the footman.

"Her father is Viscount Gilmanton?"

"Yes, the very one."

With a slight curve of his lips, Lord Knoxbridge shook his head.

"Then I would advise you to avoid that particular young lady unless you wish to have an impoverished father-in-law seeking you out to ask you to clear his debts."

"Oh?" Henry's spirits immediately dropped. "Though that is not particularly fair on the young lady. I am sure she cannot help her father's circumstances, and to marry such a young lady might bring her *out* of such difficulties rather than force her to linger within them."

"I would be very cautious in that regard." Lord

Falconer, appearing quite serious, sat forward in his chair, a sharp look in his eyes. "To be wed to a young lady is one thing, but you are also tying your families together. There can be a lot of influence brought to bear and, should your wife's father tell her of the distress he is in, I have no doubt that she would then go and speak to you without hesitation! And one can find it very difficult to refuse one's wife... or so I hear."

A little surprised at the vehemence in his friend's voice, Henry held Lord Falconer's gaze for a few minutes, only for his friend to shrug and sit back in his chair.

"My own good father was in such a situation," came the short reply. "It has taken me quite a few years to bring our finances back into a stable position, simply because of how much he was encouraged to give. I do not want the same for you."

"I appreciate your concern. All the same, I will not set her aside, not as yet anyway." Gesturing with one hand, Henry tried to smile, ignoring the twisting worries in his heart. "And I have Lady Isabella to think of also, though her mother is much too domineering."

"And she is daughter to an Earl," Lord Mallory remarked, a scowl forming. "Earls like to have their daughters wed to those of equal title."

"All the same, I must have a little hope!"

Henry tried to laugh, only for the sound to catch in his throat as he realized his hand no longer bore the one thing that he considered precious.

His father's talisman ring.

"Whatever is the matter?" Clearly aware of the change in Henry's demeanor, Lord Falconer sat forward again, eyeing Henry carefully. "You have gone very pale indeed!"

"My ring... my father's talisman." Choking the words

out, Henry turned his hand over and back again as though, somehow, that might bring it back to his hand. "It is gone."

"Gone?" Lord Falconer frowned. "What do you mean?"

"It is no longer on my hand." Setting down his glass, Henry rose to his feet and began to look all about him. "Mayhap it slipped from my finger and–"

"You think it might be somewhere here?" Standing, Lord Falconer began to help Henry with his search, as did the other two gentlemen. "I did not think it was particularly loose on your finger."

Henry ran one hand through his hair, his breathing quick.

"It does not slip off, but nor is it too difficult to remove. I do not understand what has happened to it!"

"Could it be that you lost it at the ball, perhaps when you were dancing?" Lord Mallory asked, shaking his head as he looked all around the floor. "I do not think it is here."

"Nor do I." So saying, Lord Knoxbridge sat back down in his chair, letting out a sigh. "Might it then be at Lord and Lady Chamberlain's townhouse? On their ballroom floor?"

Henry closed his eyes and let out a low groan. If his talisman ring was on the ballroom floor, then the chances of finding it again were very slim indeed.

"Mayhap one of the servants will have found it," Lord Mallory said, sitting back down. "One of them will hand it back to Lord Chamberlain and then return it to you, I am sure."

"In which case, I should take myself back to the ball at once," Henry muttered, raking one hand through his hair again as his eyes continued to search the floor for any sign of the ring. "Do excuse me."

"I can come with you if you like?" Lord Falconer began to come after him, but Henry shook his head.

"Thank you, but there is no need. Pray that I find it, however!"

Lord Falconer nodded, and Henry walked out quickly, his own heart desperately hoping that the talisman ring would soon be found.

~

"I DO APOLOGIZE, Lord Yarmouth, but I have not heard of it nor seen anyone with it." Lord Chamberlain put a hand on Henry's shoulder for a brief moment. "But if any of the servants see it, you can be assured that we will return it to you at once."

Henry nodded.

"I thank you." His stomach dropped, his shoulders heavy and his eyes downcast. "It was a desperate hope to think that it might have been found."

"But sometimes desperate hopes are fulfilled as this one might soon be," Lord Chamberlain told him, smiling encouragingly. "Pray, do not give up hope."

"Lord Yarmouth?"

Turning his head, Henry looked into the face of a young lady. With her red curls and sharp green eyes, he recognized her, though he could not quite remember her name. Excusing himself, he turned away from Lord Chamberlain and made his way a little closer to the lady.

"Yes?"

"I believe this is yours."

Henry's eyes fell to what she held in her hand, only for his breath to hitch, tightening in his chest as he took in his father's talisman ring. Staring at it for a few seconds as if to make certain that it was truly there, he reached out and grasped it, holding it between thumb and forefinger before replacing it on his hand.

"I believe that, at this juncture, it is customary to thank the person who has found your ring."

Lifting his head, Henry caught the glint in the young lady's eye, the way her lips flattened, and felt himself a little embarrassed.

"Of course. Forgive me, I am truly grateful for you delivering this back to me. I have been very worried about its whereabouts ever since I realized it was missing, and to see you standing here and holding it was... well, it quite took my breath away!" Smiling, he looked down at his hand again. "It is astonishing to see it sitting so as though it had never gone missing. You cannot know how grateful I am to you for finding it."

"I would have thought that, with such an item meaning so much to you personally – as well as it being worth rather a lot – you would have taken a good deal more care of it."

Henry blinked, unused to being spoken to so.

"I - I did take care of it."

"Not enough," came the reply. "Perhaps it would be wiser to leave it at home the next time you are to dance. Clearly, it slipped from your finger when you danced with some young lady."

In an instant, the situation which had brought the two of them together in the first instance came racing back to Henry's mind and he snatched in a breath, his eyes flaring wide.

"*We* danced together, did we not?" Was it just his eyes deceiving him or did her shoulders slump a little? Heat billowed in his face, and he looked away, realizing now that he had made it quite apparent that until this moment, he had not remembered who she was. "Might I ask for your name? I do not think I recall it."

"You did not ask for it." With a toss of her head, the red-haired young lady's eyes sharpened, cutting into Henry. "You were much too busy using me to hide from someone else."

"Which you aided me in very well indeed." A little uncertain as to what to say, which might make the young lady appear more contented than she was at present, Henry cleared his throat gruffly. "I... I was very appreciative of your help."

"I am certain that you were. You avoided the young lady you were attempting to hide from, though you ought to have been truthful with her also."

A slight curl tugged at Henry's lip.

"Yes, you have said such a thing to me once already."

Whoever this young lady was, she was certainly very forward, very willing to share her opinions and her considerations without even being asked for them.

But then again, said a quiet voice in his conscience, *you share your own opinions quite readily and no one ever asks you for them either. Why should it be different for this young lady?*

"As regards my name, I am Miss Bosworth. My father is Viscount Halifax, though it is my mother here with me in London at present."

Henry glanced around in case Lady Halifax was standing near her daughter so that he might introduce himself to her as well, but there was no one else present. It was only himself and Miss Bosworth standing together in one corner of the ballroom, talking in what would appear to others to be a most discreet manner.

A flame of warning ran down his spine.

"No, my mother is not present," Miss Bosworth sighed, rolling her eyes, and making Henry frown at such a gesture. "Ever since I have been deemed a wallflower, she seems to have decided that she should enjoy the Season and leave me to stand by the side of the room with the other wallflowers. So no, you will not find her present here, Lord Yarmouth, though the other young ladies are nearby. It is just as well that I saw you coming to talk to Lord Chamberlain! I was not certain how I would find you otherwise."

The longer she spoke, the more Henry seemed to remember about her. He recalled the flashing of her eyes as they had danced, the firm way in which she had spoken, and then, as his eyes widened, he recalled speaking of a Miss Bosworth before they had ever had the opportunity to meet.

"You were the one who spoke to Lord Dartford!" Miss Bosworth's expression flattened. Her lips pulled tight, her eyes narrowed just a little, and she nodded, turning her gaze away from his. "Oh, but I have been discussing you a great deal!" Henry exclaimed, making Miss Bosworth's expression darken. "It was the reason I stepped away from another young lady, for I found her opinions much too unfavorable."

Miss Bosworth sniffed.

"So, you speak about me as every other gentleman and lady in London has done, then? It is only that you did not know my name until this moment. No doubt, if you *had* asked for my title and been given it, you would not have asked to dance with me and would have instead, gone back to the lady you were attempting to flee from instead of standing up with me."

Hearing the tightness in her voice and seeing the gentle flush in her cheeks, Henry quickly shook his head, a little concerned now that the young lady was thinking ill of him.

"I have done nothing of the sort, Miss Bosworth. When I say I have been speaking of you, it has been to defend you."

The narrowness of her eyes began to fade as she looked back at him.

"Is that so?"

Catching the slight tone of disbelief, Henry nodded fervently, not quite certain why he wanted her to believe him but determined to have her do so regardless.

"Yes, it is. I do not think it fair that Lord Dartford can say whatever he wishes to you and you, when you say the same thing to him, are the one pushed aside."

Miss Bosworth tilted her head just a fraction, looking at him in silence for a few minutes, as though she had to ascertain in her own mind whether or not he could be trusted. Henry said nothing, looking into her eyes and keeping his gaze steady in the hope that she would soon believe him.

"I do agree with you." Speaking slowly, Miss Bosworth frowned, looking away. "I am not certain why a young lady stating that she would not be drawn to a particular gentleman is any different to a gentleman saying the very same to her! Lord Dartford was very rude in his manner, and in how he spoke to me, it seemed quite right to me to return his rudeness with a similar response."

"Though he would have been quite shocked at your audacity to do so."

Miss Bosworth snorted and looked away.

"As was his mother, supposedly."

Wincing, Henry sucked in a breath.

"Lady Dartford is known to be a prolific gossip."

"Yes, so I have heard." Miss Bosworth sighed. "And thus, I have had to deal with the consequences of treating

Lord Dartford with the same disdain as he showed to me, while nothing whatsoever happens to him."

"Something I think to be *most* unfair."

This time, when Miss Bosworth looked at him, there was no hint of distrust in her face. Instead, her expression seemed to soften and, after a few moments, she smiled.

"I think you very genuine in your remarks, Lord Yarmouth."

"I mean every word," he said, earnestly. "I do not think that you ought to be pushed to the back of society, living only in the shadows, and gaining nothing from all that society has to offer you. It is not fair."

Miss Bosworth smiled and for the first time, her eyes no longer seemed sharp. Instead, they were gentle, warmth held there instead of ice, and Henry found himself smiling back.

"No, it is not fair, Lord Yarmouth, but I have no intention of doing as society dictates that I must," she said, speaking a little more quietly now. "I am afraid I shall not be a very good wallflower."

"Then permit me to aid you in that."

Quite where this desire had come from, Henry was not certain, but his desire to aid the lady was genuine indeed and thus, he continued.

"It would be as a way of thanking you for finding my talisman ring," he said, seeing her bite her lip. "And because I do not agree with what society has said of you."

Her laugh was unexpected but when it came, it filled the air around him with light, and Henry's heart lifted suddenly.

"I am afraid that I am *precisely* as society has said of me, Lord Yarmouth." With her laughter fading to silence, Miss Bosworth shook her head. "I am *much* too outspoken. I am blunt, and forward, and do not behave as a young lady ought. You need not ask me what I am thinking on *any* occasion, Lord Yarmouth, for I will have already told you."

Red came into her cheeks, but Henry smiled, wanting to reassure her all the same.

"I do not think that those traits are worthy of such punishment." Spreading out his hands, he lifted his shoulders and let them fall. "For we do not treat gentlemen in such a way, and they are also meant to be considered, not speaking out of turn and always with consideration, is they not?"

"I... I suppose that is true." Miss Bosworth appeared a little uncertain of herself for what was the first time in their conversation, and Henry caught himself just before he put one hand out to hers, ready to grasp her fingers in what he had hoped would be a reassuring way. Where had such a desire come from? That would not be at all appropriate! "And now I should take my leave." Miss Bosworth lifted her chin and looked back again, her confidence and poise returning quickly. "I should find my mother and take my leave, for I have no intention of lingering here at the ball without a friend or companion!"

"It is near the end of the ball regardless," Henry said, with what he hoped was a reassuring smile. "Though I should be glad to step out with you to dance at whatever ball we both find ourselves at!"

Miss Bosworth's eyes caught his and in the next moment, a blossoming smile spread right across her face.

"That would be very kind of you, Lord Yarmouth, though you ought to be aware of what might happen to your reputation, should you do so." Her smile began to fade, and she turned away. "I do not think it would be wise to stand up with me again."

"Miss Bosworth, wait, please."

She did not. Instead, she lifted one hand in farewell and walked away from Henry directly, leaving him standing to look after her with a dull, unsettling feeling of discontent lingering deep in his core.

His association with Miss Bosworth was not one he was going to pull himself away from. It had only just begun and, as he looked after her, Henry's determination to aid her in whatever way he could began to grow.

This was not the end of their connection. It was only the very beginning.

CHAPTER SEVEN

"He was very grateful, yes."

A slight shift in her stomach had Joy wincing, though she kept her expression clear for her friends.

"He also told me that he disagreed with all that society had done as regards pushing myself away." Biting her lip gently, she shook her head. "I am not certain whether I ought to believe him or not."

"Why would you think he was lying?" Miss Simmons frowned, gesturing to the ballroom. "All of these gentlemen and ladies would tell you outright that they agreed that your position is now one of a wallflower. How does it serve Lord Yarmouth to lie?"

"I – I do not know." It was not something that Joy had considered before and, now that she was faced with such a question, the answer did not come easily. Why would Lord Yarmouth lie to her? What would be his purpose in doing so? The more she thought of it, the more Joy realized that there could be no purpose in his stating mistruths, not unless he wanted to try to make her feel better about her circumstances – but why should he do that? They were not known to each other. They were not even friends, so there could be no reason for him to attempt to make her a little more hopeful.

"Mayhap he was only being kind after I returned his talisman ring." Joy shrugged. "He did not want to be unkind after I had brought it back to him and thus, he hid his true opinion."

Miss Fairley, who had been leaning back against the wall, laughed and shook her head.

"You must stop thinking poorly of every gentleman who comes to speak with you, Joy," she laughed, coming to stand next to Joy, one hand going to her shoulder. "Lord Yarmouth might very well simply be a good-hearted, kind gentleman who spoke as he did because that is his true opinion."

"Perhaps." Joy allowed that to settle into her mind, considering Lord Yarmouth and his eager expression as he had spoken to her. He was a handsome gentleman, certainly, with his somewhat sturdy stature, his brown hair brushed to one side of his forehead, and green eyes, so similar to her own and yet so very different at the same time. They were darker than hers, with flickers of light and dark seeping into them, and how she had struggled not to stare up into his eyes!

And why is it that I am thinking of them – and of him – even now?

"I will consider that thought," she said, trying to take her attention away from the memory of Lord Yarmouth. "Though whether his offer to stand up with me again is to come to fruition, we shall see!"

"I do not think you will have to wait for long."

Lady Alice's voice carried loudly and clearly across

towards Joy, making her start in surprise as she turned around, only to see Lady Alice nodding in one specific direction. Turning her head, Joy's breath caught as none other than Lord Yarmouth strode directly towards them all.

"And here I was thinking that wallflowers were meant to stand at the back of the room!" Bowing, he beamed at Joy who was ready to give him a set-down for his rude manner, only for Lord Yarmouth to continue. "I am delighted to see you all standing in amongst the crowd, for that is just where you ought to be. You ought not to hide yourselves away, and I should be glad to dance with each and every one of you, should you desire it."

A flood of warmth pushed its way into Joy's heart as she heard one or two quiet exclamations from the other wall-flowers. Soon, Lord Yarmouth was signing his name to every dance card he was given, though Joy kept herself back, waiting until the last and not wanting to push herself forward. Surprised at the faint hint of jealousy curling through her like smoke, she turned her head away and looked out across the ballroom. There was no need for her to feel anything of the sort, she told herself sternly, for though Lord Yarmouth was introduced and acquainted with *her*, it would be good for each one of her friends to have at least one dance filled on their dance card.

"And last we come to you, Miss Bosworth." Lord Yarmouth smiled warmly and reached out one hand. "Might I take your dance card also?"

"But of course. Thank you." She smiled at him when he took the card from her. "And thank you for doing this. I do not think I can truly express to you how much this will mean to everyone."

Lord Yarmouth said nothing, writing his name down on her dance card and then handing it back to her.

"The country dance?"

"Thank you."

Joy smiled and slipped the dance card back on her wrist, ignoring the slight twinge of disappointment that she was not to dance the waltz. Having expected Lord Yarmouth to move away once he had finished speaking with her, Joy was a little surprised when he lingered, his hands clasping behind his back and a slight smile on his face.

"I did not ask you where you found my ring."

"I beg your pardon?"

The smile on Lord Yarmouth's face dropped.

"When you returned my ring to me, I was so overcome with delight and astonishment that I did not ask you where you discovered it."

"Oh." Joy tipped her head a fraction, studying his face, taking in the lines that had formed across his forehead as the light in her heart slowly turned to shadow. "I do hope, Lord Yarmouth, that you are not suggesting that I *stole* it?"

Lord Yarmouth paused, then shook his head.

"No, I–"

The pause before he had spoken made Joy's heart explode with a sudden, fierce anger that burned right through her, tearing at her very soul. How dare he think that she was responsible for it?

"I found it on the floor of the ballroom and, in full view of everyone, stopped to pick it up," she began, fiercely, stepping closer and pointing one finger at his chest, all the while glaring up at him. "My friends can attest to it. It is only good fortune that had me realize that it belonged to you. How you can stand there and suggest that I took it from you without you knowing is–"

"I was not going to say that you stole it."

Lord Yarmouth reached up and took her hand in his

and such was the shock of his action, Joy fell quite silent. The warmth of his fingers pressing hers sent gentle ripples up her arm until she felt her anger begin to quieten, begin to press down, and pull away from her heart.

"I did not ever think that you had stolen it," he said again, albeit all the more gently. "It was only to say that there was a concern in my heart that *someone* had attempted to take it from me, though I then stopped myself, realizing that such an idea is quite preposterous!"

Joy blinked, flames beginning to burn up her chest and into her face.

"I – I am sorry."

Lord Yarmouth chuckled and let go of her hand, though Joy instantly wanted to reach out and take his hand again.

"I do not get angry easily, Miss Bosworth, and I can see how my hesitation might have given you cause to think that I was saying something of you, but I can assure you, I was doing no such thing."

Feeling herself rather small, as if sinking into the floor, Joy closed her eyes briefly and then took in a deep breath.

"I ought not to have spoken so quickly, Lord Yarmouth. Forgive me."

"There is nothing to forgive," he told her, quickly. "It is a strange circumstance, that is all."

"In what way?"

Her embarrassment fading, she looked back at him carefully, watching how his expression changed as he spoke. His eyebrows dropped low, his hands fell back to his sides, and he shook his head, a sigh eliciting from his mouth.

"My talisman ring is an expensive item. I believe the diamond alone is worth a great deal. My father handed it down to me as one of our family heirlooms, and I have kept it safe and secure as best I can – though it does not appear that I have done so on this occasion, I admit!" His smile tipped his lips and he looked away. "I wear it on occasion and have delighted in it, I confess, but it is not a ring that can simply slip from my finger. It does not take a great deal of difficulty to remove it, however, but it has never once fallen from my hand before now."

"And thus, you believe that someone took it from you? How could they do so?"

Lord Yarmouth hesitated, then shook his head again.

"I do not know. My only thought was that it might occur during the waltz?"

"Oh." Joy's heart clattered in her chest. "You mean, a young lady could have taken it from your hand as you danced? That would have taken some care, would it not? I would think it very difficult."

A sudden brightness came into Lord Yarmouth's expression, his eyes flaring.

"Should you like to try to do so?"

Joy frowned.

"I – I beg your pardon?"

"During the country dance," he explained, moving a little closer to her now as his voice became a little higher due to his excitement. "When we dance, I shall do my very best to focus solely on the dance and you must do your utmost to take the ring from my finger."

Laughing, Joy waved one hand at him.

"You are teasing me."

"No, I am not! I should be very glad if you would be willing to try to do so."

Realizing that he was quite serious, Joy studied him for a few seconds then let a smile spread right across her face.

"Very well, Lord Yarmouth. If you wish me to attempt to steal your talisman ring from you, then I shall do so.

Though I hope it will not affect my reputation in any way, should anyone see me try to do so!"

Lord Yarmouth chuckled, his eyes bright.

"I can assure you that everyone will be so busy dancing, they will barely take notice of us! I admit that now, I am rather excited about the country dance."

"Let us hope I am successful," Joy replied, her heart quickening a little at the grin on Lord Yarmouth's handsome face. "The only trouble is, then you shall have to attempt to work out who it was that might have taken the ring from you."

A little light faded from Lord Yarmouth's face, and he took in a breath before shrugging his shoulders.

"Let us see what happens, Miss Bosworth, shall we? I can consider what I am to do next, should you be able to take the ring from my finger."

Joy nodded, her mind whirring as she thought about what she was going to do and how best to go about stealing the ring from Lord Yarmouth's hand. This dance was certainly going to be one of the most interesting dances she had ever taken part in!

THE MUSIC CONTINUED and a light sheen of sweat broke out across Joy's forehead. They had been dancing for a few minutes already and still, she had not once been able to grasp hold of Lord Yarmouth's ring. Whenever their hands came together, she had barely had time to even think about what it was she had to do before he stepped away again.

A little frustrated, Joy focused all of her attention on the ring and, remembering that the dance would bring them closer again, determined that she would do her best to take the ring from his hand. Stepping closer, their hands joined, held down low by Lord Yarmouth's side and, as she began to step away, Joy tightened her fingers and, with a broad grin, felt the ring slide from the gentleman's finger.

She was unable to catch it, however, and, letting out a small exclamation of dismay, looked all around for it while, at the same time, attempting to keep to the dance.

"Have no concern, I have it."

Joy let out a breath of relief as Lord Yarmouth came close to her again, the dance slowly coming to an end. Taking her hand, he bowed low over it and then, smiling, stepped back. Dropping into a curtsey, Joy smiled at him as she lifted her gaze to his, a gentle flush rising in her cheeks.

"I am relieved that you have the ring safe. I do not know what I would have done had it fallen to the floor again!"

Lord Yarmouth nodded and then offered her his arm.

"Mayhap that is what happened. Someone tried to pull the ring from my finger and though they succeeded, they did not manage to catch it." Joy took his arm and walked alongside him, a slow frown growing as she considered what he had just said. "Was it very difficult to manage?"

"It was," Joy admitted, speaking slowly as she let a few thoughts run around her mind. "However, once I focused all of my attention upon it, I did succeed... in part."

Lord Yarmouth nodded.

"Then it seems that someone might have attempted to steal the ring from my hand during our dance. That seems very strange, however, for–"

"There is another consideration." Aware that she had interrupted him, Joy stopped, turning to face him, her hand sliding from his arm. "Forgive me. What was it you were saying?"

He smiled at her.

"Nothing that cannot wait. What were you thinking of?"

Joy hesitated, letting her thoughts come into complete clarity before she began to explain.

"There is another explanation, as I have said, one which does not require there to be some ill will or desire to steal."

"Oh?"

Her shoulders lifted.

"It could have been an accident."

Lord Yarmouth frowned.

"An accident?"

"Yes, an accident." Aware that he was frowning, Joy paused again but then permitted herself to speak openly. After all, she had always done so, and simply because she was in Lord Yarmouth's presence did not mean that she ought to stop herself now. "A glove might have caught on the diamond and pulled the ring from your hand. When it is hot – as it always is during dancing – then it is more than likely that the ring simply slipped off. I am not certain I would seek to put the blame on anyone specific, or even start questioning which young lady you had danced with on one particular night!"

A sigh broke from Lord Yarmouth's lips.

"Yes, I suppose that is a wise consideration." Making himself smile, he spread out his hands. "But all the same, it was good to see that it *could* have happened that way. Though I think that your considerations are more than likely what took place."

"Thank you, I appreciate your willingness to listen to me." Joy smiled at him and when he let his gaze linger, when he smiled back at her, her heart filled with a gentle warmth that did not fade with any swiftness. "I – I suppose I should go back to my friends now."

"We shall dance again, I hope?" Without warning, Lord Yarmouth reached out and took her hand, his eyes searching her face. "Even if you are a wallflower, as you say, I do not see any need to hide yourself away. Besides which, I very much enjoyed our dance, as I did with all of your friends also."

This last sentence stole away the joy which had been building in Joy's heart. With a nod and a smile, she stepped away and made her way back across the room to where the other wallflowers were standing. No longer standing in the dark, swathed in shadow, they all watched her return and Joy forced a smile she did not feel onto her lips. For whatever reason, Lord Yarmouth's remarks that he had enjoyed each and every dance with Joy's friends was burning a hole in her heart – and despite telling herself that she should be nothing more than delighted that he had danced with all of them, all Joy could feel was a burning jealousy, which grew hotter with ever second which passed.

CHAPTER EIGHT

Henry tilted his head, turning his father's ring over and over in his fingers, his forehead knotted, and his mind filled with questions – none of which he could answer immediately.

Was Miss Bosworth correct? Had the loss of his ring been a mere mistake? Or had there been a deliberate attempt to take it from him?

I do not know why someone would do that... aside from the obvious monetary value.

Pursing his lips, Henry rubbed one hand across his forehead and set the ring to one side of his desk. It was a family heirloom, so who would be trying to take it from him?

A knock at the door had his thoughts pushed to one side as he called for his butler to enter.

"Yes, Lawson? What is it?"

The butler came forward, handing a card to Henry.

"My Lord, you have a visitor. He claims to be your cousin."

"My cousin?" Henry frowned, rising to his feet. "He has come to call?"

"Yes, that is so. A Mr. Brackwell, I believe."

A sudden memory came back to him, and Henry nodded.

"Yes, Simon Brackwell. I remember him." Pushing his chair back, he came around from his desk. "I will go to the parlor - please have him shown there."

The butler nodded and stepped out of the room, leaving Henry to hurry after him, so that he might make his way to the parlor before his visitor – but he did pause to turn the key in the door of his study and then set the key in his pocket. At the moment, that heirloom was much too precious to be lost again, and Henry did not want to leave it in an unlocked room, even though there was no one nearby who might take it.

Stepping into the parlor, Henry wandered to the window and clasped his hands behind his back, waiting for his visitor to be shown in. From what he remembered, Simon Brackwell had been sent to a boarding school in Wales, and just before that had been the last time they had seen each other. He himself had been sent to Eton at the tender age of seven, as was right for a son of a Viscount, and, over the years, he had forgotten entirely about his cousin, save for a letter some years ago, stating that Mr. Brackwell had gone to the continent to secure his late father's holdings.

It is to my shame that I have forgotten about him.

At that very moment, the door opened, and the butler ushered a gentleman in.

"Mr. Simon Brackwell, my Lord."

"But of course." Striding forward, Henry put out one hand and took the man's hand, taking in his features. There were some similarities between them, what with the brown hair and green eyes but, aside from that, Henry did not see much else. Then again, he considered, shaking his cousin's hand firmly, he could barely recall his uncle! "Brackwell, how are you?"

"I am grateful that you allowed me to simply walk into your house and call upon you," came the reply, as he smiled broadly. "I know this must be something of a surprise."

"It is, but it is a pleasant one," Henry replied, quickly. "Please come in and sit down."

"I thank you." Sitting down, Mr. Brackwell looked around him, taking in everything in the room. "This room has a most pleasant aspect."

A little surprised at how refined this gentleman was, Henry thanked him and then sat down, nodding to the butler that a tray with coffee and cakes should be brought in.

"You were on the continent, or so I heard."

Mr. Brackwell nodded, looking at Henry again.

"Yes, I was." There came a slight frown upon his face as he spoke, though his words thereafter explained his expression. "My father begged me to go to the continent on his behalf, and make certain that all of his holdings were quite secure, for there had been a few skirmishes reported. He was a little unwell and I confess, I did not want to go, but both he and my mother begged me to do so. Thus, I took my leave of England, but once I was there, I received a letter only a month later stating that my father had passed away."

Henry's heart grew heavy, recalling the passing of his own father.

"I too was also away from home when the news came of my father's passing," he said, seeing Mr. Brackwell's eyes widen. "It was not as far as the continent of course, but all the same, the pain was great. I wished I could have been there with him."

"Then we have that in common," Mr. Brackwell murmured, rubbing one hand over his chin. "It took me far too long to return home, and by then, the funeral had already taken place. I comforted my mother and sister as best I could – though thankfully, my sister was already wed by that time – and once I had made certain that my mother was well cared for, I returned to the continent to continue my business there. The small estate my father handed down to me was left to the care of my mother until my return. I took my pain and grief with me, however."

"My sympathies."

Mr. Brackwell nodded his thanks, only for the door to open and the trays to be brought in. Henry took the chance to study his cousin, taking in the lines around his eyes and the hints of grey through his hair. They were both of similar age, but it appeared that the sorrow and sadness of losing his father had taken its toll on the man's appearance.

"So," Henry continued, once his cousin was sitting with refreshments to hand, "what is it that brings you to my door?"

With a smile, Mr. Brackwell shifted in his chair to make himself a little more comfortable.

"In truth, it was in the hope of becoming a little better acquainted with you. Yes, we are cousins, and so we are family, but we do not know one another very well at all. I have come to London on business, but I do not know anyone here in the city, save for an old friend who lives a little nearer to the East End than I would like!"

Henry winced.

"I understand."

"I am not asking for you to introduce me to your friends or the like, or to bring me to any of the society events which you attend," Mr. Brackwell continued, hastily, waving one hand. "I do not want such a thing, for I am not of your class or standing, but–"

"But that does not make you any less a gentleman," Henry interrupted as Mr. Brackwell smiled in obvious appreciation. "I would be glad to introduce you to one or two of my friends, even though you say you have no wish to be introduced. I am certain that they would be very glad to meet you. It would bring you a little more companionship to be sure, and that is only a good thing." Rather touched by his cousin's desire to recover their connection – one which had been broken since childhood – Henry leaned forward in his chair and nodded fervently. "Yes, I think that must be the way forward. It will help you in your connections here in London – and indeed, might do so when it comes to busi-ness also – and my friends are of a good sort. They will be more than welcoming, I assure you."

After a few moments, Mr. Brackwell nodded.

"Very well." There was still a hint of hesitancy in his voice, but Henry only smiled, sure that his cousin's wariness would fade quickly. "Mayhap I shall speak to them about crop rotation and the like! The estate is a good deal smaller than yours, of course, but it still requires the same care."

"I am certain that they will all be very glad indeed to speak with you about whatever you wish," Henry told him, a smile on his face as his cousin reached for another cake from the tray. "I am glad that you have returned to London. It will be good for us to grow our connection again. We have so very little family, I do believe that such connections are important." His smile began to dim as the realization that he had not been doing anything to encourage his connection to his cousin and his family filled him. "I should like to do whatever I can for you, Brackwell."

"I appreciate that, more than I can say." There was a

warmth in Mr. Brackwell's voice now, a familiarity in the way he spoke which Henry was certain came from their connection as children. "Mayhap this connection will bring me into the sphere of a young lady! My mother insists that I marry soon." Chuckling, he rolled his eyes, then steadied his gaze again. "Thank you, Lord Yarmouth."

"Not at all." With a nod, Henry took a sip of his coffee and then set the cup back down again. "I look forward to introducing you to them all."

$\approx$

"You say he is your cousin?"

Henry nodded as he and Lord Falconer sat down in the corner of White's and watched as Mr. Brackwell continued with his prolonged conversation with Lord Knoxbridge. They had begun to discuss crops, and what the fields were growing at this present moment, and seeing that he was no longer needed to facilitate a conversation, Henry had stepped away.

"My father had only one brother. He was born only ten months after my father, and I believe that they were very close. He married and had two children, Brackwell and his younger sister. She is already wed, from what Brackwell said, and now he is the one caring for the small estate his father left to him."

"And you have not seen each other in some time?"

"Not since I went to Eton and he to Wales," Henry replied, with a shake of his head. "But I am glad he thought to come to my townhouse and speak to me about it all. It will be good to establish our connection again. And mayhap he will find a young lady to marry also, which would be all the better! I believe his mother has been urging him to do so."

Lord Falconer's grin spread slowly as he turned his full attention to Henry again.

"And what of Miss Bosworth?"

A frown flickered across Henry's forehead.

"What about the lady?"

"You have danced with her on two occasions. You have danced twice with a wallflower!"

Henry shrugged.

"That does not mean anything in particular."

"Are you quite certain of that?" Lord Falconer chuckled when Henry frowned. "It has been known, on occasion, for a wallflower to catch a gentleman's eye."

"She has not caught my eye." A stab through his heart made Henry shift uncomfortably. "Miss Bosworth *has* been treated unfairly, however, and I am determined not to do the same as the other gentlemen and ladies of the *ton*."

"A most worthy ideal," Lord Falconer agreed, "but that does not mean you need to dance with her as frequently. You must like the lady."

Henry considered for a few moments, aware that Lord Falconer was still grinning.

"I think her conversation most stimulating, and I confess that, while she is a little more blunt that some – if not all – of my other acquaintances, I do not consider that to be a great difficulty. In fact, I have found her considerations to be very wise indeed, especially when it comes to the loss of my ring."

Lord Falconer's grin cracked apart.

"Yes, your ring! What did you discover?"

"That my ring *can* be slipped from my finger during a dance, though Miss Bosworth confessed to losing it once she had managed to take it from me. Much to my relief, I had spotted it and was able to collect it as we danced.

"That *is* good." Lord Falconer frowned. "So, does that mean that you believe that someone attempted to take the ring from your finger, then? That it was a deliberate act?"

"I am not certain." Henry clicked his tongue, a light frown on his face. "Miss Bosworth thought that it might have been an accident. Mayhap a glove became caught and accidentally pulled the ring from my finger. Miss Bosworth considered that such a thing could have occurred and therefore, there was no one specifically to blame."

Lord Falconer nodded slowly, one hand at his chin.

"That is an idea, I suppose. All the same, you should be cautious. There may be someone out there who wants that ring for themselves."

"But why?" Henry asked, spreading out his hands. "What possible reason could someone have for taking my late father's ring? Yes, it could bring them some coin, but surely there are easier things to steal!"

"I do not know."

"Perhaps I am being foolish, keeping it locked away. I do not feel quite myself when I do not wear it."

A flash of light caught Lord Falconer's eyes.

"Though mayhap you should discuss it with Miss Bosworth again, since she has been of such a help to you already. Perhaps she will have some more thoughts on the matter, and can share them with you." Henry said nothing, choosing not to rise to Lord Falconer's remarks. "Oh, or you could introduce her to your cousin!" Lord Falconer exclaimed, making Henry's frown grow all the deeper. "She is a wallflower, he a gentleman – yes, without a title but a gentleman all the same – and mayhap they would make a good match!"

Something fierce threw itself at Henry's stomach and his gut twisted, his expression tight. The thought of Miss Bosworth and Brackwell being introduced was not exactly an unpleasant one but, all the same, his aversion to the idea was significant and strong. Without realizing it, he shook his head slightly, and Falconer obviously noticed.

"No?"

Scowling at the light smile on his friend's face, Henry pushed himself out of his chair, ready to end the conversation.

"I think it is time for me to take my leave," he said, aware that he was being a little abrupt. "Good evening, Falconer."

His friend's grin did not fade.

"Good evening, Yarmouth."

Henry nodded to his cousin and then took his leave, stepping out into the cool evening air and feeling the brush of the wind against his cheeks. Walking towards his waiting carriage, he dropped his head and scowled down at the street as though somehow, it was responsible for the strange turmoil going on within him at the present moment.

Lord Falconer was quite correct, he *should* introduce Miss Bosworth and Mr. Brackwell for the match might be a very good one, even though Brackwell held no title. But all the same, Henry could not even *think* of the idea without a sharp, unexpected pain lancing right through his heart and thus, silently to himself and without understanding or explanation, he determined that he would never permit such a situation to occur, no matter how much he knew he ought to do so.

CHAPTER NINE

"I do not know what we are to do."
Joy sighed.

"Mama, there is nothing to be done, save for what I, and my friends, have determined to do."

"Which is causing whispers and rumors to fly about London!" Lady Halifax exclaimed, her voice a little too loud for Joy's liking. "Whoever heard of wallflowers walking through ballrooms, laughing and smiling together and even dancing!"

"Those things are perfectly acceptable, Mama." Refusing to let herself begin to feel even a hint of guilt over what she had begun to do, Joy lifted her chin a notch and looked straight ahead as they walked through St James' Park together, though she had not taken her mother's arm. "Wall-flowers are permitted to walk about together. They are allowed to laugh and smile and even to dance, should a gentleman ask them!"

Lady Halifax groaned, her head dropping forward, though Joy remained unmoved.

"Must you always be so difficult?"

A sharp pain pressed into Joy's heart, and she looked away, tears beginning to burn behind her eyes.

"Mama, I am not doing such a thing because I am being difficult, as you put it. I am doing such things because it is so very unfair. There is no reason for either myself or my friends to have been pushed back in the way we have been, no reason for us to be told to cling to the shadows. I refuse to accept that, refuse to believe that it is what I must now expect. Therefore, I will stand tall with my friends, I will walk about with them and prove to the *ton* that we have as much right to be in amongst them as they do."

"I wish you would not."

"Then what is the alternative for me?" Turning, she stopped walking and faced her mother, who had immediately begun to shake her head, not looking Joy in the eye. "What is there to be done? You do not even walk with me during the ball or soiree, should we be invited to one. Instead, you go in search of your own friends and leave me quite alone!"

"What am I to do other than seek out a little enjoyment for myself? I have failed in securing you a husband... no, *you* have failed by making certain that no gentleman wants to consider you."

Joy swallowed at the knot in her throat.

"Lord Yarmouth has stood up with me on two separate occasions now."

"Because he is a soft-hearted fellow who has taken pity on *all* the wallflowers," came the acid reply, Lady Halifax's eyes narrowing. "I have watched him dance with everyone, yourself included. Do not think that it means anything, or that he has some genuine interest in you. Clearly, his heart is concerned for all of you, and he is doing what he can to show you a little interest in the hope that it will be an encouragement."

Joy did not think that her mother's words were meant to wound with such fierceness but, all the same, they cut with great strength and soreness. Ever since she had first spoken to Lord Dartford and, thereafter, dealt with the consequences, her mother's attitude towards her had changed significantly. Instead of compassion and understanding, there had been a growing hardness, a desire to pull away, rather than support. Keeping her gaze fixed straight ahead, she narrowed her eyes just a little in an attempt to keep the tears from filling them, refusing to let a single one fall. She was strong. She was determined within herself, for that was who she was and what she had clung to. To permit herself to be molded into something else, into *someone* else, as her mother had desired would not have brought her any happiness.

But neither does this situation.

"I do not know what we are to do." Lady Halifax let her heavy sigh fall in Joy's direction. "Mayhap I ought to take you back home but then that would mean an end to the Season... and I do not think that I am quite ready to return. There may still be a *slim* chance that someone might consider you, though–

"There is no need to return home," Joy said, firmly, her voice cutting through her mother's words. "I have no intention of turning away from what I am doing at present, however. My friends and I will continue to behave as everyone else does at balls and soirees. I will not be pushed to stand in the shadows."

"Then *no one* will consider you!" Throwing up her hands, Lady Halifax began to stride away from Joy, just as she did at every occasion which they attended together. "I thought that perhaps a gentleman without any hope of a match might look to a wallflower, or one who lacks any confidence whatsoever would consider someone even quieter than he, but now, if you continue to act as you have been, then what will become of you?"

Joy blinked furiously to keep her tears back, wondering if her mother had even the slightest idea of just how much her words hurt. It was as though the only thing she cared about was marrying Joy to anyone who would have her, rather than carefully considering precisely who such a person was, and what sort of husband they might be to Joy.

I am truly saddened by all of this. Dropping her head, Joy took a deep breath. *My mother has never been at all sympathetic, and now I feel almost entirely alone.*

Taking another long breath, Joy lifted her head and began to follow her mother – drawing even more attention to herself at the present moment would not be favorable.

"Are you quite all right?"

Joy blinked in surprise.

"I–"

"Forgive me for interrupting you, I ought not to have done so. Indeed, I am sure that I should not even be *speaking* with you, since we are not introduced but, given that I am not one of the titled gentry, perhaps the requirement does not apply."

"It is not usual to speak so to a lady, particularly when one has not been introduced, but I myself am not always entirely eager to stay close to all that propriety demands!" Joy found herself smiling, taking in the man's somewhat eager expression. There were hints of grey running through his hair, but his eyes were kind and Joy warmed to him immediately. "I am well, I thank you."

"That is good." He gestured to the path. "Are you walking this way?"

"I am. My mother is a little ahead of me."

"Then might I walk with you? I confess that I do not know very many people here in London, and I have only just now passed a distant cousin of mine, but she did not wish to speak to me."

"Oh?" Joy frowned, silently wondering if there was something about this gentleman that she ought to be wary of. "And why is that?"

The man smiled, his eyes twinkling.

"She was walking alongside a gentleman – her secret beau, from what she whispered to me, and thus you find me quite alone! I would be glad of a little company."

On hearing this, Joy did not have even the smallest hesitation.

"But of course. Might I enquire as to your name?"

The man nodded, a small flush creeping up his neck.

"Of course, forgive me. I am Mr. Simon Brackwell."

"How very good to make your acquaintance," Joy answered, as she began to walk down the path with Mr. Brackwell beside her. "I am Miss Joy Bosworth. My father is Viscount Halifax though my mother is with me in London at present."

"I am glad to meet you. I thought to take a walk through the park on my way to return to my lodgings."

"Do you live in London?"

The gentleman shook his head.

"No, my estate – small though it is – is in the north of the country. My mother resides there at present, and my sister, who is married and settled, lives nearby with her husband. They are all very contented I believe, though it is I who must make my way to London to do business and thus, miss the beautiful spring days that are to be had in the countryside!"

"Ah, but London has a great many enjoyable occasions and the like," Joy countered, wincing a little as she spoke, knowing full well that she had nothing else good to say about London society, given how it had treated her thus far. "You must attend a ball or some such thing and that, I am sure, will help you forget about what you are missing back at your estate."

Mr. Brackwell chuckled, his hands held behind his back as they walked.

"Perhaps I shall, though quite how I am to be invited, I cannot say!"

Joy smiled at him.

"I will find one or two acquaintances to introduce you to and then, you will simply *have* to be invited," she said, quickly trying to think about who it was she might introduce Mr. Brackwell to. It ought to be someone who would not think less of him simply because he held no title, someone who had kindness and consideration within them. "Though I will admit that my acquaintances are few and far between, given that society deems me to be a wallflower and nothing more."

"Oh?" Mr. Brackwell frowned. "I do not see how that could be fair."

"It is not." Biting her tongue, Joy held herself back from speaking any further on the subject, aware she ought not to allow herself to linger on the matter. "However, I am afraid, therefore, that my connections are rather few. I may not be the ideal person to introduce you to others, but I shall do my best!" To her mind came none other than Lord Yarmouth and she smiled suddenly, looking up at Mr. Brackwell. "Wait a moment, I recall one gentleman to whom I should introduce you! He has been most kind and has not treated me, or my friends, as wallflowers, as every other gentleman and lady has done." Mr. Brackwell nodded at her, his eyes alive with a sudden interest. "He is Viscount Yarmouth," Joy continued, quickly. "I do not know him particularly well, but I would say that he is a very kind, considerate fellow who would be more than glad to speak with you."

Much to her surprise, Mr. Brackwell laughed aloud, catching her mother's attention. Lady Halifax turned around sharply and quickly began to stride back towards Joy, clearly now concerned that this gentleman was behaving in an untoward manner.

"I must say, he will be glad to know that you think so highly of him." Putting out both hands, Mr. Brackwell then let them fall as he smiled. "Lord Yarmouth is my cousin."

Astonished, Joy's mouth fell open, only for her mother to reach her and, grasping her hand, gave her a gentle tug back. She did not take even the smallest bit of her attention away from Mr. Brackwell, however.

"Your cousin?" she echoed, as Mr. Brackwell nodded fervently. "Goodness, how very interesting!"

Her face grew hot as she wondered whether Mr. Brackwell would truly tell Viscount Yarmouth about what she had said of him.

"I only just came to London and, hearing his name mentioned, thought to seek him out," Mr. Brackwell explained, quickly, glancing at Joy's mother and seeing the hard look in her eyes. "Good afternoon, Lady Halifax. I was just speaking to your lovely daughter about our common acquaintance, Lord Yarmouth. He is my cousin."

"Oh."

Joy glanced at her mother and was forced to hide her smile. Her mother had clearly been ready to snap out a sharp response, only for Mr. Brackwell's charming introduction to have taken some of her wrath away.

"Mr. Brackwell was so good as to stop to make sure that I was not alone."

"If you had walked alongside me rather than dawdling behind, then you would not have looked as though you were lost!"

Lifting her eyebrows, Joy watched with interest as her mother turned scarlet, clearly mortified by how sharply she had spoken to Joy in front of a new acquaintance. With a forced smile, Lady Halifax turned her attention back to Mr. Brackwell and let out something which was, Joy considered, meant to sound like a laugh, but was somewhere between a cough and a croak.

"I only hurry my daughter because we are due to have dinner in a short while," she said, by way of explanation. "I am sure that you understand."

Mr. Brackwell smiled and threw a look at Joy, who smiled back at him.

"Of course I do. Dinner is the most important meal, I am sure, as is whatever plans you have for the evening thereafter!

"We are to attend Lady Ralston's ball." Joy could not keep from rolling her eyes though thankfully, her mother did not notice. "An opportunity to make new acquaintances, though I do not think any will look upon me with any favor!"

"Then they do not know you in the least," came the firm reply. "From what you have told me, I do not think it fair that you have been treated in this way, though they are seemingly determined to do so."

"You are most kind, Mr. Brackwell, but alas, we must take our leave."

With a curtsey, Lady Halifax took Joy's hand and led her further along the path, with Joy only able to look backward over her shoulder to Mr. Brackwell. With a smile, she lifted her hand in farewell and, when he returned the gesture, Joy was filled with a wonderful, coursing happiness which did not leave her for the rest of the day.

CHAPTER TEN

"*L*ord Yarmouth?"

"Come in." Henry stepped back from the window, turning around just in time to see none other than Mr. Brackwell stepping inside. "Cousin!" he exclaimed, coming closer and shaking Brackwell's hand. "How good to see you!"

"I thank you."

Gesturing to the couches, Henry indicated that his cousin should sit down.

"How marvelous to see you. It has been near a sennight, has it not?"

Making his way across the room, he poured brandy for them both and set one in front of his cousin on a small table near to where he sat.

"I believe so. It is only a short time to be in London alone but, all the same, I have found it to be a friendly, welcoming place. I have been very busy with all manner of business affairs most days and have spent the evenings doing very little other than resting! Today I am a little more at liberty, however."

Ringing the bell, Henry took his seat and smiled at his cousin.

"I am very glad to hear it. I have Lord Falconer coming to call very soon, and I should be glad if you would join us if you have time to linger?"

"I do have a little time."

"Capital!" Exclaiming aloud, Henry sat forward in his chair. "Tell me about all you have been doing – where you have been, who you have met, and the like. I would like to hear all about it."

"Well, I had the most interesting conversation with a young lady yesterday afternoon." Tipping his head, Mr. Brackwell lifted his eyebrows, as if he wanted Henry to guess. "She was in the park, quite alone, I thought, and standing very still indeed, as if something was wrong. I went to speak with her, and she and her mother were walking together – though it did not appear like it, at first."

Henry nodded but said nothing, wondering which young lady he spoke of.

"We began talking and though I had not been formally introduced, she was very eager to speak with me – and more than willing to aid me in my desire to make new acquaintances. She thought nothing of my lack of title and said to me that one person she could think of, one who would not mind about my lack of title, who was very kind, generous, and considerate was none other than you yourself!"

Surprised, Henry sat back, looking at his cousin with wide eyes.

"Is that so?"

"It is! She thinks very highly of you, I must say."

"So it seems." Uncertain of who it was that Mr. Brackwell could be speaking about, Henry frowned. "Who was this young lady?"

A little fearful that it might be Lady Judith, he held his breath, only for his cousin to laugh.

"You need not look so afraid! It was a Miss Joy Bosworth and, from how she spoke of you, it seemed as though you were well acquainted."

A breath of relief escaped Henry and he smiled, though his heart filled with an unexpected warmth as he thought of the young lady.

"I am glad to hear that it was she, and not some other, that is all!" he explained, as his cousin laughed. "And you say that she spoke well of me?"

"*Very* well. Is she connected to you in some way?"

Henry shook his head.

"Not in any particular way, no." Seeing the gleam in his cousin's eye, Henry's frown quickly returned, though he fought to remove it from his expression just as quickly as he could. "That is to say, we are acquainted, and she has been a great aid to me in one or two matters, but that is all."

"I thought her a very lovely young lady, though her mother is a little overbearing and somewhat condescending." Mr. Brackwell's smile broke away at the edges as he turned his eyes away. "It is as though Miss Bosworth was to blame for lingering behind her mother when I thought Lady Halifax ought to have turned around to make certain that her daughter was with her. If she had, then she would have noticed that her daughter was upset."

Concern flared and Henry sat up a little straighter.

"What was the matter with her? What was the concern?"

"She did not say. In fact, she reassured me that she was quite well."

"Oh." Sinking back down, Henry chewed on the edge of his lip, not seeing the curious way his cousin watched him. "It must be exceptionally difficult to be a wallflower, I think. Though I confess that in the few Seasons I have been present in London, I have not always taken notice of them."

Mr. Brackwell nodded.

"It does seem strange that someone so vibrant might be considered nothing more than a shadow. I will be glad to see her again."

"You have made an arrangement, then?" Trying to disguise the sudden twist in his stomach by keeping his voice light, Henry's hands tightened around the arms of the chair as his cousin nodded. "That is... good."

"Would you like to join us?" Mr. Brackwell smiled and reached for his glass of brandy. "We thought to walk in the park again the day after tomorrow."

It was as if a hand clasped around Henry's throat as he considered. The truth was, he had no desire to linger in his cousin's company, should he be making endeavors towards courting Miss Bosworth. Given the severe amount of discomfort he was in at present over the very idea of it, the thought of being present and watching their connection grow stronger was a painful one.

"I think... oh, do excuse me."

Hearing the tap at the door, Henry called for the butler to come in, only for Lord Falconer to stride in ahead of the man.

"Lord Falconer, my Lord."

"Yes, I can see that." Grinning – and rather relieved that he did not have to answer his cousin's question – Henry quickly made the introductions, "Falconer, you remember my cousin, Mr. Brackwell?"

"Yes, of course I remember!" Lord Falconer boomed, shaking Mr. Brackwell's hand firmly and then walking to where the brandy stood. "A measure for myself, I think."

Sitting back down, Henry chuckled as Lord Falconer poured himself a large measure and then came to join them.

"As you can see, Brackwell, Lord Falconer is a very dear friend, for he knows that he can help himself to my brandy without even a question!"

Lord Falconer chuckled and soon, a conversation struck up between the three of them. Many questions were asked, much laughter abounded and much to Henry's relief, the topic of Miss Bosworth did not return to his cousin's lips again.

~

"DID you enjoy your dance with Miss Gilbert? I hear she is looking for the very richest of husbands."

Henry rolled his eyes.

"Then I am not the right gentleman for her."

"No, you are not." Lord Falconer chuckled as Henry grinned. "By the way, I think your cousin is a fine fellow."

Henry, trying to catch his breath, could not resist a little mockery.

"Is that because he told you repeatedly how much he admired your willingness to try new methods when it came to your fields and crops?"

Lord Falconer grinned, his eyes glinting.

"Mayhap. Though, I did wonder…"

His smile faded and he frowned, though his eyes remained on the crowd rather than returning to Henry. Waiting for some minutes, Henry sighed aloud when his friend said nothing, elbowing him lightly.

"Ouch!"

"Well?" Henry arched an eyebrow. "Tell me, what is it that you wanted to say?"

"It is only that I did wonder if he had anything to do with the ring?"

A line drew itself between Henry's eyebrows.

"The ring?"

"Your father's talisman ring," Lord Falconer explained, sounding a little exasperated as he finally looked at Henry. "Could he have some use for it? After all, he has his own estate, but it sounded to me as though he was struggling with all the financial matters once his father died."

Henry shook his head.

"I believe that there was some difficulty, yes, but it has since been resolved. He has worked hard and gleaned the benefits of it. Besides which," he finished, as Lord Falconer nodded solemnly, "he was not present in London – or at the ball – when the ring disappeared."

Lord Falconer's shoulders dropped.

"That is true enough, I suppose. I had forgotten that."

"So no, he could not have been responsible or even involved in the attempted theft of it, if that is what it was." With a sigh, Henry shrugged. "I do not know what to make of it all. I think for the time being, I shall forget all about it and–"

"Where is your ring this evening?"

Henry blinked, lifted his hand and stared at his fingers – all of which were entirely without rings. Lifting his ring hand, he looked at his signet ring, thinking that perhaps he had placed the talisman ring on the right hand instead of his left but again, it was not there.

"Oh, no."

"It is lost *again*?" Lord Falconer threw up his hands. "Then it *must* have been your cousin. He–"

"It cannot have been him," Henry interrupted, grasping his friend's arm in an attempt to quieten him. "It was on my finger this evening before I left for the ball. My cousin has not been invited to this ball and I have danced at least five dances already tonight."

Lord Falconer rolled his eyes.

"Why did you continue to wear it? If you knew that there was a chance it might be pulled from your finger – whether by accident or deliberately – then why wear it again?"

"Because... because it has been a few days since the first happening and I told myself I was being a little ridiculous." Hearing that his excuse sounded weak, Henry closed his eyes tight and winced. "It seems as though I should have left it at home, however."

"I remember you saying that you did not feel quite like yourself without it, but I did not realize that meant you had thoughts of wearing it again. I thought you would have kept it safe until the mystery had been solved."

"I did not think there *was* any mystery!" Groaning, Henry rubbed one ringless hand down his face. "I believed it had slipped from my hand accidentally. Except now... now it seems that I have had it taken from my hand."

Lord Falconer nodded.

"Yes, it does seem so. I do wonder who has done such a thing and why." His eyes glittered. "You say you have danced five dances already?"

Henry nodded, not understanding his friend's questions.

"Then you know the ladies you danced with." Speaking slowly as if he were explaining things to a child, Lord Falconer spread out both of his arms wide. "Those are the young ladies you must suspect!"

Blinking, Henry's eyes flared.

"I must suspect them of stealing my talisman ring?"

"Why not? That is what would make the clearest sense, would it not? You must look at them, one by one, before attempting to understand what has taken place and why. *That* gives you the beginning of solving this mystery."

Henry's stomach knotted. He did not want to even think that one of the young ladies he had danced with had taken his ring from his finger but, then again, if he had no one else to consider, then his friend was right, they were the most likely.

"Except," he said slowly, wincing as Lord Falconer frowned, "for two of the dances, I was in amongst the other dancers, moving between them and, on occasion, turning a different lady to the one I had stepped out with."

"Oh." Lord Falconer's voice lost all excitement. "That is rather difficult, then."

"Yes, it is."

Taking in a deep breath, Henry looked out across the ballroom, taking in as many faces as he could and wondering just who would have taken the ring from him. The lights from the candles seemed to grow dim, darkness creeping into the edges of his vision as his spirits sank low.

Where was he meant to go from here?

CHAPTER ELEVEN

*J*oy's heart sank as she watched Lord Yarmouth walk across the ballroom without so much as a glance in her direction. It seemed as though she and her friends had been quite forgotten by the gentleman and, though she told herself that she ought not to expect attention from him, there was still disappointment lingering in her spirit.

"Who is it that you have been watching so carefully?" Miss Simmons came to stand next to Joy and quickly, Joy tugged her gaze away from the gentleman in question. "You need not be afraid to tell me, it is not as though I am about to speak of it to anyone else."

Her gentle voice and kind expression had Joy's eyes swelling with sudden tears, but she kept them back, refusing to permit herself to give in to any emotion as pertained to Lord Yarmouth.

"It is foolishness and nothing more," she said, aware that Miss Simmons' eyes were searching her face, concern lighting them. "I had thought... I had *hoped* that there might be something more to Lord Yarmouth's interest in the wall-flowers, but it seems there is not."

Miss Simmons smiled gently.

"I understand. He did seem to be a very kind gentleman and indeed, I still believe that he is. No doubt some other young lady has caught his attention, and that is to be expected."

Because a gentleman, such as he, would not look at a wallflower.

Her heart ached terribly, and Joy looked away, embarrassed by her strong reaction. She had only danced with the gentleman on two occasions and yes, she thought him handsome and kindhearted to the point that her thoughts *had* become a little tangled up with him of late.

"I think I shall walk around the ballroom again." Taking in a breath, she set her shoulders and tried to push all of her feelings as regarded Lord Yarmouth away. "Should you wish to join me?"

Miss Simmons chuckled.

"If you are to be bold then I think I can be too!"

Joy smiled at her.

"You still feel a little reluctant?"

Miss Simmons' smile faded.

"Yes, I confess that I do. It is rather unusual for a wall-flower to step out in the way that we do, and I am aware of the interest that we have garnered. That being said, I am determined not to be held back, for you are quite correct when you state that the *ton* can do nothing more to us! I am already a wallflower with very few hopes, and nothing can be gained from standing at the side of a room, desperate for even *one* gentleman to look at me. No, in this regard, I am a good deal more determined than I have ever been before."

Joy's heart softened.

"I am glad to hear you say that. My mother has been less than pleased to see me behave so."

"And I am sorry for that. We have all been grateful for your encouragement and for your determination to push us forward. That has been the greatest help to me." Offering Joy her arm, Miss Simmons smiled warmly. "Let us continue as we have planned. The *ton* shall know that we are here this evening, just as they are."

Joy nodded and, with a broad smile, took Miss Simmons' arm and began their promenade around the ballroom. Her friend was right. Even if Lord Yarmouth was not to show her even the slightest interest, that would not make a singular bit of difference to her determination to remain as present as she could be, in amongst the *ton*. Though all the same, said a quiet voice, did she not hope that, in doing so, Lord Yarmouth might take notice of her again?

～

"I – I DO NOT BELIEVE IT!"

Without warning, Joy came to an immediate stop, staring at a small, dainty object that lay on the floor only a few steps away from them. Both she and Miss Simmons had walked around the ballroom not once but twice and yet now, as they were about to return to their friends, Joy's eye had caught on something more unexpected.

"What is it?"

"Look!" Joy nodded with her chin, then dropped Miss Simmons' arm. "I cannot understand what it is doing here!" Hurrying forward, she bent down quickly and picked up the gold talisman ring with the one single diamond in the center, holding it up for Miss Simmons to see. "That is the very same ring I picked up from the floor that night of the ball, when we first determined to step out together. Do you recall?"

Miss Simmons let out a small exclamation and came hurrying forward, her eyes rounding as she looked at the ring.

"Good gracious, so it is!"

"It must belong to Lord Yarmouth." A frown pulled at Joy's forehead. "Though quite what it is doing here, I do not know. How can it have fallen from his hand again?"

"It must be larger than he believes," Miss Simmons suggested, as Joy shook her head. "No?"

"I have attempted to remove it from his hand during the dancing." Explaining quickly what had taken place, Joy did not look at her friend for fear that she would see something in her eyes, something which told her that there was more in her heart for Lord Yarmouth than she was willing to express. "It was incredibly difficult and, even though I was successful in the end, the ring fell to the floor. I know for certain that it is not too big, given how much effort I had to put in as I attempted to do what we both suspected might have happened!"

Miss Simmons took the ring from her and looked at it again, her eyes sharpening.

"There is a crest on it. I do wonder if..." Frowning, she looked to Joy. "You believe, then, that someone attempted to take it from Lord Yarmouth's hand during the dancing?"

"It was one suggestion." With a pause, Joy shrugged. "I did suggest to Lord Yarmouth that, given how difficult it was for me to do, his ring had perhaps fallen from his hand by accident. Now, however, I begin to believe that there is more to the situation than there first appears. Why would his ring have fallen from his hand *accidentally*, twice in a row?"

Miss Simmons' frown grew.

"It would not have done. This must have been a deliberate act."

"But why? Why would someone seek to steal a ring such as this – and to attempt to do so for a second time?"

"For the diamond and the gold?" A twist of Miss Simmons' lips told Joy that she was not entirely convinced herself about this. "It would bring in a little coin, certainly."

"But not a great deal." Joy rubbed one hand over her eyes, trying to think clearly. "The crest might have some significance, I suppose?"

Miss Simmons nodded.

"Perhaps." She looked back to Joy. "Are you going to return it to him?"

Joy nodded.

"Of course. I shall simply have to find him first!" Turning, she looked around the ballroom but, in the crowd, could not see him. "I shall have to go walking through the ballroom again, in search of him."

"Or..." Miss Simmons tilted her head, a fresh light coming into her eyes, "or you could wait."

When she smiled and giggled, Joy frowned, not understanding.

"What do you mean?"

"Precisely that!" Still smiling, Miss Simmons leaned a little closer. "You shall have to call upon him, tell him that you have found something of significance and *that* is your reason to call. He will, no doubt, invite you to take tea and then that will be all the better!"

Joy hesitated, a nervousness beginning to snake around her stomach. While she could see why Miss Simmons had suggested such a thing, she felt herself immediately pulling back from it. To go to call upon a gentleman was not something that was usually done, and certainly not by a wallflower!

But I am telling all of my friends that we are not to cling to such a name, she reminded herself, as her friend waited. *Am I now to go against that?*

"You have a better acquaintance with him than the rest of us." Miss Simmons spoke quietly as if she were able to see just how many thoughts were running through Joy's head and did not want to interrupt them. "I think he would be glad to see you."

"Yes, but only because I have the ring."

"Perhaps for another reason also." Miss Simmons smiled as Joy blushed furiously, looking away again. "I know that you think well of him. Perhaps there is a desire for more within you? You seek to further your acquaintance with him and therefore, you are a little concerned when I suggest such a thing given your feelings at present – but you need not be. I think it would be good for you to go and call upon him. It would remind him of you." Joy dropped her head, aware of just how hot her face had flushed. How had Miss Simmons known of her interest in Lord Yarmouth? She had never spoken of it but yet, her friend had clearly become aware of it. "If you wish to go and find him now, however, I will go with you." With a warm smile, Miss Simmons tilted her head and studied Joy. "Do not be embarrassed, my dear friend. It is quite reasonable for a young lady such as yourself to have an interest in a gentleman like Lord Yarmouth."

"Except I am a wallflower."

Miss Simmons lifted her shoulders and let them fall.

"That may not matter. After all, he has shown himself to be interested in your company already, has he not? Come, do not be disheartened. Go to call on him and see what happens thereafter."

With a quiet huff of breath, Joy built up her courage and nodded fervently, looking back to her friend with a smile.

"Very well. You have convinced me."

"I have?" With a laugh, Miss Simmons wrapped one arm around Joy's shoulders and hugged her tight. "Wonderful! I am sure that your visit will go very well indeed, for he will certainly be incredibly grateful to you. After all, this will be the second time that you will have not only found but returned his ring to him."

"Let us hope so." With a smile, Joy set the ring in her reticule, pulled the reticule strings tightly closed, and then patted it gently. "And if all goes poorly, then I know exactly who to blame."

Laughing, the two ladies fell into step together and continued with another walk around the ballroom, walking arm in arm. For the first time since she had come to London, Joy felt herself excited, anticipating what was to come, and wondering what it was that could happen once she returned the ring – for the second time – to Lord Yarmouth.

❧

"Good afternoon."

Joy cleared her throat and looked up at the butler.

"Good afternoon. I am come to call upon Lord Yarmouth. Is he at home?"

"He is."

Seeing the butler glance behind Joy, clearly looking for a chaperone or someone similar, Joy stiffened as she stepped inside, relieved that the butler had not pushed her out of the house directly given that she only had a maid.

"I must speak to him at once," she said, a little stiffly. "It is a matter of urgency."

The butler nodded and much to her relief, took her bonnet and gloves from her without a word of protest.

"Of course, my Lady. Might I ask who is calling?"

"Miss Bosworth."

With another nod, the butler gestured for her to follow him, and with a breath of relief, she did so. Walking with her head held high and ignoring the swirls of nervousness that ran through her continually, she clasped the ring tight in her hand and followed the butler.

"Lord Yarmouth and Mr. Brackwell are together in the drawing room," he said, gesturing to the door. "Please, permit me a moment to announce you."

Glancing at her lady's maid and nodding that she should follow her, Joy waited as the door was opened and then, closing her eyes against the swell of anxiety in her stomach, followed in after the butler.

"Miss Bosworth has come to call, my Lord." The butler cleared his throat, gesturing to Joy. "It is a matter of urgency."

"Urgency?" In a moment, Lord Yarmouth had crossed the room and, much to Joy's surprise, caught her hand in his, his eyes searching her face. "Whatever has happened?"

"It is nothing terrible, Lord Yarmouth, though I thank you for your concern." Joy did not remove her hand from his but smiled instead, seeing the relief that flooded into his face, light washing over his expression as he let out a breath of relief and then smiled. "And do excuse me for interrupting your conversation with Mr. Brackwell." So saying, she smiled and inclined her head to Mr. Brackwell, who had also removed himself from his chair though he had not rushed over as Lord Yarmouth had done. "How nice to see you again."

"And you. If you desire to have a conversation with Lord Yarmouth alone then I can easily take my leave."

A sudden flurry of excitement rushed through Joy, but she quickly shook her head, knowing it would not be wise to sit alone with Lord Yarmouth, even with her maid.

"I thank you for your concern but there is no need. Please, do feel free to linger." Her eyes went back to Lord Yarmouth. "It has to do with the ball last evening."

Lord Yarmouth squeezed her hand.

"I am sorry."

"Sorry?" Joy's eyes widened as she saw him frown. "Whatever for? From what I saw, there was nothing that you did that was wrong."

"I did not come to speak with you and nor did I dance with you." The regret that tinged Lord Yarmouth's voice had Joy's eyebrows lifting in astonishment. Did he truly feel so much regret over not standing up with her? "I had every intention of doing so, but a situation took place which caught all of my attention and, I confess, I did not dance a good many dances thereafter."

Mr. Brackwell cleared his throat before Joy could say anything more and both she and Lord Yarmouth looked at him quickly.

"I do wonder if you might like to sit down, Miss Bosworth?" Mr. Brackwell said, pointedly, as Lord Yarmouth let out a low exclamation and then dropped his head forward in clear embarrassment. "You have been standing for some minutes and though this conversation is an excellent one, I do wonder if you would be more comfortable sitting down?"

Joy laughed as Lord Yarmouth began to stammer an

apology, squeezing his fingers gently before letting his hand go, still wondering at the closeness of their touch.

"I should like to sit, yes."

"And let me call for a tea tray," Lord Yarmouth said quickly, going to ring the bell. "My apologies, Miss Bosworth. I ought to have been the one to offer you such a thing and instead, I have my cousin making certain that you are comfortable rather than myself!"

"It is just as well you are here, Mr. Brackwell." With a teasing note in her voice, Joy smiled broadly as she sat down again, making Mr. Brackwell laugh aloud. "Else I should be departing from this house in both fatigue and thirst!"

"Indeed, you would, and we could not have that." Mr. Brackwell grinned as Lord Yarmouth sat down again, though Joy noticed the slight flush to his cheeks. "Now, I believe that you were in the middle of an apology – *another* apology, I might add – to Miss Bosworth?"

Thankfully, Lord Yarmouth laughed at this, as did Joy herself, and Mr. Brackwell sat back in his chair, arms folded but a grin still plastered on his face.

"Indeed, I was." Clearing his throat, Lord Yarmouth gestured to Joy. "As I was saying, a situation occurred last evening which took all of my attention. It was that which kept me from greeting you, though I assure you, I had arrived intending to do so."

Joy smiled and nodded, clasping her hands in her lap.

"Might I ask, Lord Yarmouth, if this situation had to do with your gold talisman ring?" The shock which spread across Lord Yarmouth's face was unmistakable. His eyes rounded, his mouth fell open, and his gaze fixed on hers. "The reason I ask," Joy continued when he said nothing, "is because last evening, I happened to come across something that danced on top of the ballroom floor."

Lord Yarmouth closed his eyes, one hand going to rake through his hair.

"It cannot be."

His hoarse voice made Joy smile.

"I am afraid it is, Lord Yarmouth," she said, pulling the ring from her pocket and holding it out to him. "Last evening, I found the very thing you had lost... for the *second* time. Your father's gold talisman ring."

CHAPTER TWELVE

*I*t was as if the air had been pulled from the room, leaving his lungs burning and his face hot. Staring at Miss Bosworth's hand, his gold talisman ring settled in her palm, Henry could do nothing but gaze at it, hardly able to take in what it was that she held out to him.

How much had he cursed himself last evening when he had realized that his ring had fallen from his hand for the second time? He had spent most of the evening thereafter looking for it, wandering around the ballroom in search of it, though he had not asked the host to announce its loss for fear of the embarrassment it would bring. Eventually, he had given up hope, afraid now that he had lost it forever or that whoever had managed to take it from him would now keep it in their possession for the rest of their days.

And now, Miss Bosworth held it in her hand, as though she were holding out a gift to him.

"You lost your ring?"

It was Mr. Brackwell's puzzled voice which broke through Henry's reverie and, nodding fervently, he took it from Miss Bosworth and closed his eyes in abject relief.

"You cannot know what this means to me." Aware of the hoarseness in his voice, Henry closed his eyes tightly, his throat working. "I shall never take this out of this house again."

"Perhaps that would be wise." Miss Bosworth smiled at him gently, her eyes soft. "It seems that someone is eager to take this from you."

"Indeed it does."

Mr. Brackwell cleared his throat, then smiled apologetically when they both looked at him.

"Forgive me for the interruption, I am just attempting to make certain that I understand. Did someone take this from you? Your father's talisman ring?"

A little surprised that his cousin remembered the ring, Henry nodded.

"That is so. It initially was lost at a ball some days ago now, though Miss Bosworth was the one who found it for me."

"And then you found it again?" Mr. Brackwell blinked. "That is a surprise!"

"It is."

Was it just to his own mind or did Miss Bosworth look suddenly a little uncomfortable? Henry shrugged inwardly and then quickly reassured the lady, aware that while it was surprising to know that Miss Bosworth had found the ring not once but twice, he did not think anything of it. It was pure luck, that was all... even if his cousin believed differently.

"It was a stroke of luck having your sharp eyes spy it," he said, glad when a small smile spread across Miss Bosworth's features, making her green eyes a little more vivid. His stomach dropped at the beauty of her, only to rise back up again as his heart slammed hard against his ribs, leaving him struggling for breath.

"I am glad to be able to return it to you, that is all. I can assure you, Mr. Brackwell, that I did not have any involvement in Lord Yarmouth's loss of this ring, however." Still struggling to catch his breath, Henry watched with a little amusement as his cousin's face flushed a bright red, clearly a little embarrassed that, not only had the lady understood what he was thinking, but she was now as bold as to speak of it directly. To his mind, Miss Bosworth was certainly direct, but he did not see that as a failure of personal character. It was... refreshing. "I did not take it from Lord Yarmouth's hand only to return it to him, then do the very same thing again. There would be nothing to gain from such a thing."

"Save to catch his attention." Still crimson red, Mr. Brackwell shifted in his seat, only to close his eyes tightly as though he had only just realized what he had said. "Forgive me. I did not mean–"

"Miss Bosworth would not have to do a single thing to catch my attention, other than look in my direction."

The moment that he spoke those words, Henry's heart jumped so high that he began to cough, ruining what otherwise might have been a very significant moment. His cousin offered to fetch a glass of water, Miss Bosworth herself sat forward, with the appearance of concern, but Henry waved his cousin away, managing to regain himself but at the very same time, hot with embarrassment. He had meant those words, but he had not meant to say them with such fervency! Much to his relief, the tea tray was brought in, and he was soon able to push away his mortification, silently praying that Miss Bosworth did not think he had not meant them, due to his coughing and spluttering in the moments thereafter.

"So, do tell me about your family, Miss Bosworth." Mr. Brackwell settled back in his chair as the lady gestured to the tea, looking at Henry with an expectant smile.

"If you wish to serve the tea, then please do so." Henry sat forward. "But there is no requirement nor expectation of it. I can pour if required."

Miss Bosworth laughed and assured him that she was quite able to pour the tea though, when her laughter faded, her gaze and her smile did not. Instead, both lingered, the former clinging to him as though she did not ever want to look away – or was doing her utmost to form a memory of him in this moment that would never fade. Henry smiled back at her, his heart still pounding a little more quickly than usual, though he wondered at the reason for it. Yes, his words had been genuinely meant, but was it that he truly did care for Miss Bosworth? They had not spent a great deal of time together but, all the same, Henry had to admit to himself that there was a flickering interest within him, nonetheless. She was outspoken, bold, and determined, and yet, despite knowing that such qualities were not encouraged in young ladies, Henry found himself rather admiring her. She was not acting as any wallflower had done before and truth be told, even that was intriguing.

"And so you are the last to marry."

Henry blinked, realizing that, having become lost in his thoughts, he had missed the entirety of the conversation between Mr. Brackwell and Miss Bosworth.

"Yes, I am the last, though my mother now despairs for me." Miss Bosworth's smile fell as she handed Henry his tea, though she quickly returned it to her face thereafter. "I am much too bold in my words, it seems, and have managed to push myself into the situation of being a wallflower. Thus, my mother has decided that I am no longer able to garner even the smallest amount of attention from any gentleman whatsoever and spends most of her time at the various occasions we are invited to with her own friends and companions."

Mr. Brackwell frowned.

"It is not a situation I am at all familiar with, but it does sound rather difficult. I am sorry for that."

"And I appreciate that, though I do not regret being as I am." Miss Bosworth picked up her tea and took a sip. "I could not imagine being wed to someone who did not know my true character." Her eyes closed and she shuddered briefly, making Henry's eyebrows lift in surprise at how strongly she felt on the matter. "It would not be fair, either to him or to myself and thus I have refused to change my character for my mother's sake."

Henry's eyebrows lifted, but he found his lips tugging into a smile of approval. Miss Bosworth was determined, yes, but there was a desire to be honest and truthful there also and he appreciated and admired that. She was right; to be wed to someone who only *after* the marriage vows revealed the truth of their character would not be a blessing for either husband or wife and he valued her clear decision in that.

"I think I quite agree, Miss Bosworth. It is far better to know the character of one's husband or wife *before* the wedding."

"Should you like to convince my mother of that, I would be very grateful." Her eyes twinkled with obvious mirth and Henry laughed, shaking his head, and picking up his tea again. "Though I think I should take my leave now."

"So soon?" Before even giving himself time to think,

Henry found himself on his feet, coming towards her as though he were desperate for her not to step away from him. "You have not been here for long."

"Long enough," she smiled, sipping the last of her tea before rising to stand by him. "My mother will be wondering where I have got to if I do not return, and I do not want to add to her burden."

"You are no burden, Miss Bosworth." Without warning, without even a thought, he reached out to take her hand in his, overjoyed when she did not pull away, though her eyes held a good many questions within them. "I should be glad to have you come to call at any time."

Miss Bosworth nodded slowly and though she did not smile, her eyes flickered. Was she thinking about what he had said? Or was there something more there?

"Mayhap you would like to walk together in the park?" Much to Henry's frustration, his cousin rose from his chair and, coming across to Miss Bosworth, reached out to take her other hand as Henry dropped the one which he held, and took a small step back. "It has been wonderful to make your acquaintance and I should like to spend a little more time with you, should you be amenable?"

Mr. Brackwell spoke as though Henry was not present, interrupting what had been *his* conversation with Miss Bosworth and sending a streak of frustration running up Henry's back.

"I should like that." Miss Bosworth smiled, though her gaze ran towards Henry himself, leaving him to make the only response that seemed possible at the time, which was to shrug and smile vaguely, even though he did not like the idea of his cousin stepping out with Miss Bosworth, especially when *he* had been the one to ask in the first place. "And you will join us, Lord Yarmouth?"

"Perhaps." A little uncertain now, Henry forced his lips to curve as he looked only at Miss Bosworth and not at his cousin. "It will depend on how many business affairs require my attention on the day of your outing, though I should very much like to do so."

Miss Bosworth smiled and nodded.

"I understand. Well, should you be able to join us, then I would be very glad indeed to see you again. Thank you, Lord Yarmouth. Good afternoon, Mr. Brackwell." With a quick curtsey, she turned to take her leave, only for Henry to hurry forward and catch Miss Bosworth by the arm.

"I – I wonder if..." Whether it was the heat which ran from the room as she opened the door or his own sudden uncertainty, Henry did not know but a chill ran over his skin, making the hair on his neck stand on end as he looked into Miss Bosworth's wide green eyes. He dropped his hand. "I only wondered if you might consider taking a walk at another time." It sounded strange even to himself, but he continued regardless, hearing the buzzing in his ears as he attempted to explain himself, albeit in low tones. "I should like to walk with you. Alone. I mean, not alone, for you would obviously require a chaperone but—"

Miss Bosworth put a hand on his arm, silencing him.

"Are you asking if I should like to walk with you in the park, Lord Yarmouth? Without the company of your cousin?" Henry swallowed and nodded, his words sticking in his throat. "Then yes, of course, I should be glad to."

Relief had his shoulders dropping low.

"Capital." Throwing a quick glance over his shoulder, he saw his cousin nearby and cleared his throat gruffly, wondering if Brackwell had overheard everything. "May-hap... mayhap you might have another theory as to what might have happened to my ring on *this* occasion."

"That is what you wish for me to do when we walk together?" Miss Bosworth frowned quickly, her delighted expression quickly altering into a somewhat dull one. "You wish to discuss your ring?"

An awkwardness gripped Henry and he shrugged, trying to laugh, though the sound came out as a tight, scrawled sound.

"It would give us something to talk about, certainly! And I should like to know your thoughts."

"Oh." Miss Bosworth nodded but looked away. "I see."

"We shall discuss nothing of the sort when *I* walk with you." A streak of annoyance ran up Henry's spine and he turned sharply, throwing a frustrated look in his cousin's direction, but Brackwell only grinned. "Good afternoon, Miss Bosworth," Mr. Brackwell continued, that grin still plastered onto his face. "I will write to you very soon to arrange our walk."

"I look forward to it." Miss Bosworth looked for a long moment to Mr. Brackwell and, eventually, then to Henry. "Good afternoon, Lord Yarmouth. I was glad to return the ring to you again."

Henry nodded, his high spirits shattering. Opening his mouth to bid her farewell, he was left with the sound of the door closing as she stepped away.

Somehow, he had managed to make a mess of what had been a very simple request – and he had no one to blame for it but himself.

"She is a very fine lady," Mr. Brackwell murmured, as Henry turned around. "A wallflower, though?"

"By no fault of her own, and only due to the scourge which is society's expectation."

Scowling still – though part of it was still from what his

cousin had done in asking to walk with Miss Bosworth – Henry sat back down in his chair.

"However did you meet her, then? Do you seek out wallflowers deliberately?"

Henry rolled his eyes.

"No, I do not but, then again, I do not ignore them either."

"I understand."

Seeing the curiosity still in his cousin's expression, Henry let out a sigh.

"In truth, I was attempting to escape from not one but two young ladies. One of them you will know – Lady Judith?"

A light came into Mr. Brackwell's expression.

"Yes, our cousin. I met them all shortly before I left for the continent, and have already spoken to Lady Judith since being in London."

"Is that so?" A little surprised, Henry continued, not noticing his cousin attempting to say something more. "Well, I had no wish to dance with Miss Blakefield *or* Lady Judith and thus, I did my best to escape from them both but had no other choice but to ask a stranger to me – Miss Bosworth, as I know now – to dance the waltz with me. I did not know who she was or that she was deemed a wall-flower, but I was very glad indeed that she stepped out willingly."

Laughter broke from Mr. Brackwell and despite his own dulled spirits, Henry laughed along with him, finding his heart warming at the memory of stepping out with Miss Bosworth on the first night that they had been introduced. It had been a very odd meeting, and certainly not one he had expected, but all the same, it had brought him a great deal of happiness since then.

Happiness I should like to continue.

"She seems like a very interesting young lady." Mr. Brackwell's smile grew as he looked away from Henry, rubbing one hand over his chin. "I should be very pleased to further my acquaintance with her, I think."

Choosing to say nothing, Henry locked his frustration away, telling himself silently that he had no right to determine who it was that Miss Bosworth should stand up with, or go walking with... even if he desperately wished that *he* was the only one she would ever step out with again.

CHAPTER THIRTEEN

"*I* think I may have made an error."

Joy blinked.

"Good evening, Lord Yarmouth."

"Good evening."

The gentleman appeared flustered, his cheeks a little flushed, his gaze darting all over the place as he repeatedly pushed one hand through his brown hair, shifting from foot to foot as he did so. She was standing at the back of the drawing room as the other guests mingled, a little upset that none of her friends were present as yet. Miss Fairley was due to attend but had not appeared thus far, leaving Joy friendless and alone. Her mother had, as usual, taken her leave rather quickly and Joy's only companion, until this moment, had been the dull shadows of the room.

"What is the matter, Lord Yarmouth?"

Joy tried her best to keep a neutral expression, preventing her true feelings from showing on her face. The nearness of him – so near to her that she could feel his breath rushing across her cheek – was sending every part of

her into flurries of excitement, as though she were anticipating something wonderful.

*He may be here to tell me that asking me to walk with
him was a mistake.*

At that thought, her excitement faded almost as quickly
as it had come.

"Are you quite alone this evening?" Lord Yarmouth
frowned suddenly, his hand dropping to his side as he
looked around the room. "You have no companions? No
friends?"

"Miss Fairley is due to attend." Resisting the urge to ask
him what it was he wanted to say to her, Joy forced a smile.
"I will have a friend soon."

Lord Yarmouth clicked his tongue, his expression one of
distaste, and Joy's tension faded a little. Clearly, he was still
displeased about society pushing her away from them, and
that was something, at least.

"I will stand with you until Miss Fairley arrives, I
think." He looked at her then, beginning to stammer. "Oh,
I – I quite forgot. I was to – to say something." Closing his
eyes, he took a long breath and steadied himself, seeming
to grow outwardly quieter as he let it out again slowly.
"Miss Bosworth, it is not that I wish to walk with you
simply to talk about the disappearance of my father's
ring." Opening his eyes, he looked into her face, his voice
quiet now, a gentleness in his expression as he took a small
step closer. "That is not why I wish to be in company with
you, I can assure you of that. Forgive me for my foolishness."

"There is no foolishness to be had here, Lord
Yarmouth." A tide of happiness sent warmth all through
her, pulling the worry from her heart and washing it away.
He was not about to tell her that he did not want to walk

with her after all, as she had feared. "I quite understand that you would like to know what has taken place."

"I would, but I should also like to be in your company, simply because I wish to be... in your company." With a groan, Lord Yarmouth rubbed one hand over his face and then threw back his head for a moment. "I am not a gentleman used to expressing myself, it seems, Miss Bosworth." When he looked back at her, there was a rueful smile on his face and Joy's heart softened all the more. "Forgive me for that."

"Whereas I am much too bold in what I wish to express!" Laughing wryly, Joy shook her head and then let her hand touch his for only the briefest of moments. "I should like that very much, Lord Yarmouth, just to walk with you. Though if you would like to discuss your father's ring and the loss of it twice over, then I would be glad to do so." Her smile grew as heat flared in her cheeks, though she refused to permit herself to look away. "I confess that the mystery does capture my attention somewhat."

Lord Yarmouth's eyes flared.

"Then you think it is deliberate?"

"Yes, I do now, since it has been taken from you twice," Joy agreed, quickly. "But perhaps that discussion can wait for another time?"

"Tomorrow?" The hopeful hint in his voice had her heart catapulting across her chest. He truly was taking an interest in her, wanted to spend more time in her company... and she could hardly take it in. "In the afternoon? Unless you are already engaged."

Joy laughed softly and shrugged.

"I am a wallflower, Lord Yarmouth. It is not as though my time is precious. I think you will be the very first gentleman I shall walk with this Season, in fact!"

His brow furrowed.

"Save for Mr. Brackwell."

"Though he did not do so deliberately the first time," she reminded him, wondering if there was a hint of envy there, or if he and his cousin were simply a little at odds over some other matter, given the change to his expression. "And he has not yet written to me to arrange the time, so you are the first!"

This sent such a broad smile across Lord Yarmouth's face, Joy could not help but laugh, though he then flushed and ducked his head. When he lifted it, however, he was still smiling and Joy returned it, a silence growing between them, but one which held no tension or awkwardness. It was as if, finally, they understood each other and were contented with what each desired, given it was the same as their thoughts.

Her happiness could not have been greater.

"I am sorry for my tardiness."

Another voice came between them, and Joy jumped in surprise, turning to see Miss Fairley curtseying to Lord Yarmouth. In talking with Lord Yarmouth, she had quite forgotten that Miss Fairley was also to join her. It was interesting just how quickly all thoughts of her friend had faded from her mind.

"Good evening, Miss Fairley." Putting a smile on her face, Joy waved away Miss Fairley's concerns. "Please, do not worry. I had Lord Yarmouth for company, did I not?"

"Though I am certainly not the very best of company," Lord Yarmouth added with a smile, though his eyes lingered on Joy's. "I shall take my leave of you now. Good evening, Miss Fairley. I look forward to our walk together tomorrow, Miss Bosworth. I hope you have an enjoyable evening."

"Thank you, Lord Yarmouth. Good evening."

Smiling, Joy let her gaze linger on him as he walked away, finding herself rather excited and this time, the feeling did *not* fade.

"You have found yourself back in his company, then?" Miss Fairley leaned against her for a moment and when Joy looked, Miss Fairley was smiling warmly, her eyes twinkling. "I presume you are very glad to have been speaking with him again."

Joy let out a low groan and closed her eyes.

"Am I truly so obvious? So apparent?"

"You are," came the reply, "but I do not blame you. Lord Yarmouth did seem to show you particular interest, and I am glad that he is continuing to do so. You are to walk with him, then?"

"Yes, tomorrow. In the park." Clasping her hands tightly together, Joy fought back the swell of anticipation which threatened to overwhelm her. She wanted to clap her hands and jump up and down at the same time, such was the strength of feeling within her heart. "It is all most unexpected! I am to walk with his cousin also, Mr. Brackwell, but he has not written to me as yet to arrange it."

Miss Fairley's eyebrows dropped, her mouth puckering.

"And would you be glad of his company?"

"Of Mr. Brackwell's?" When her friend nodded, Joy lifted her shoulders. "It would be pleasant company, but it would not be of as much interest to me as Lord Yarmouth's company, if you understand what I mean."

Miss Fairley's smile quickly returned.

"I certainly do understand," she agreed, taking Joy's hand and squeezing it gently. "I do hope that all goes as you wish. Who knows? You may find that Lord Yarmouth *is* a gentleman willing to consider a wallflower."

Hope seared through her, and Joy caught her breath,

imagining herself walking arm in arm with Lord Yarmouth as they wandered through the park. Was it too much to let herself hope for? Or was she finally to find a little happiness?

~

"Whatever are *you* doing walking about here?"

Joy stopped quickly as a lady stepped directly into her path, her eyes flashing. Joy looked first to Miss Fairley, wondering if her friend was acquainted with this lady, only to see the widening of her eyes.

Evidently not.

"Good evening." Battling to hide the surge of frustration that overtook her, Joy bobbed a curtsey. "We are walking through the house, as I believe guests are permitted to do."

"But not you." The woman's lip curled. "You ought to be standing over *there* and not letting yourself be seen."

Joy was about to exclaim aloud that simply because she was a wallflower, it did not mean that she should have to stand in the shadows, only for Miss Fairley to speak up.

"And why should we do that?"

There was a note of confusion in her voice and Joy immediately smiled to herself, seeing now what her friend was trying to do. By pretending that she did not understand what the lady meant, she was forcing her to speak aloud of what she thought – and not every refined young lady would do such a thing. While society recognized them as wallflowers, very few would be as specific as to point it out directly, especially not in good company.

They would have to wait and see whether *this* young lady was such a person.

"Because that is where you are *meant* to stand." The

young lady's eyes narrowed, perhaps aware now of what Miss Fairley was trying to do. "You understand what I mean, I am sure."

"I do not think that we do. Unless dancing is about to take place and we are standing in the way?" Joy frowned and looked around her before shaking her head. "Alas, I am not certain that there will be dancing this evening."

The other young lady's eyes flashed dangerously, but Joy only smiled.

"*You* were speaking at length with Lord Yarmouth."

Joy's interest piqued. Was this the young lady's true concern, then? Was she upset that Joy had been speaking to Lord Yarmouth when she was nothing more than a wallflower?

"Yes, I was. He is an excellent gentleman, I must say."

The young lady hissed out a breath, her face red now.

"And what were you speaking of?"

Letting out a quiet laugh, Joy tossed her head.

"I hardly think that is your business, especially given that we are not friends – and not even acquainted either."

The young lady closed her eyes tightly, her hands curling.

"I am Lady Judith. You see? *Now* we are acquainted." Opening her eyes, she pointed to Joy. "Now, tell me what you were speaking of with Lord Yarmouth. He is my cousin and I have every right to know what you were speaking of. You were the one he danced the waltz with even though *I* ought to have been the one standing up with him and yet you–"

"I am not simply going to agree to tell you everything that was shared between Lord Yarmouth and I, Lady Judith, regardless of whether or not you are related." Speaking more firmly now, Joy lifted her chin a little but held the lady's gaze steadily. "It is a somewhat rude question, I must say, especially for you to demand it of me."

What the lady had said about Lord Yarmouth dancing the waltz with Joy had reminded her of that moment. It had been the first moment that they had met, the time when Lord Yarmouth had been doing his utmost to escape from Lady Judith, and Joy had aided him in that.

I almost ought to be grateful to Lady Judith for pushing him away from her and towards me instead.

"Why are you smiling? You ought to be doing as I ask! I–"

"Shall we continue our walk through the house, Miss Bosworth?"

Joy smiled and took Miss Fairley's arm, ignoring the exclamation of frustration that came from Lady Judith.

"I should be glad to." Turning her eyes back to Lady Judith, she kept her smile in place. "And good evening, Lady Judith."

Without another word – and ignoring Lady Judith's protests - Joy walked away from her company, arm in arm with Miss Fairley. It was not until they stood in the hallway between the drawing room and the parlor that they both let out a loud exclamation, talking together about the irritated, demanding young lady.

"It seems she has been watching Lord Yarmouth!" Miss Fairley's eyes rounded a little. "Do you think he is at all interested in her company?"

Joy shook her head.

"Given that he came to waltz with me instead of with her, I should say no. That was how we were first introduced; he begged me to waltz with him so that he would not have to stand up with two young ladies who were both in eager pursuit – and one was Lady Judith."

"I see. So he waltzed with a wallflower and since then, has sought out your company more and more." Miss Fairley's eyes twinkled as Joy blushed. "I have great hopes for you, my dear friend. Let us pray that your walk with Lord Yarmouth will bring you even a hint of what is to come between you. I am certain it will be quite wonderful."

"I can only hope that you are right."

Aware of the heat in her face, Joy dropped her gaze, but her lips curved into a smile nonetheless, despite Lady Judith's strange and forceful interruption. Her walk with Lord Yarmouth was only one more night's sleep away, and Joy could hardly wait for that moment to arrive.

CHAPTER FOURTEEN

*S*he is quite beautiful.

Henry smiled back at Miss Bosworth, taking her in and permitting his heart to feel all that it wished as he did so. Curls of her auburn hair were peeking out from under her bonnet and in the sunshine, the green of her eyes was all the more intense. Her lips seemed to be pulled into an ever-present smile and, as he continued to gaze at her, a gentle flush came into her cheeks.

"Forgive me." A little embarrassed, Henry lowered his gaze. "I was simply thinking to myself how fine a day it is – and how lovely you look, Miss Bosworth."

"Truly?"

The surprise in her voice had his eyes shooting back to hers as he nodded fervently.

"Yes, of course. I would not lie or pretend otherwise, I can assure you."

"Oh." It took a few moments but eventually, Miss Bosworth smiled. "That is very kind of you, Lord Yarmouth. Thank you for such a generous compliment."

"It was not generous at all. You deserve many more compliments, I think." With a smile, he offered her his arm and felt his heart leap when she took it without hesitation, and they set off, her lady's maid behind them, a few steps away. "I am very glad to be walking with you, Miss Bosworth."

"As I am also." Her head tilted towards his, her eyes searching his face as they began to walk through St James' Park. "Your cousin also wrote to me. We are to walk tomorrow."

Henry's heart fell back into place.

"Oh."

"I have accepted, of course... unless there is some reason that I ought not to do so?"

With a sigh, Henry shook his head.

"No, there is no reason to refuse him. Mr. Brackwell is an excellent gentleman and, though he has had some trials, he has worked very hard to resolve them, and now his estate is doing marvelously because of it."

"You speak very well of your cousin."

Henry nodded, wishing that he did not have to talk of his cousin, not when he was walking arm in arm with Miss Bosworth. He did not want her to think well of Mr. Brackwell, to think highly of him. Instead, he wanted Miss Bosworth to think only of himself rather than being eager to discuss another gentleman.

"He is a good fellow, I think. I do not know him very well, but from the time we have spent together this Season, I would think he is an excellent man."

"Then he could not have taken the ring from you?"

With a jolt of surprise, Henry turned his head to look at Miss Bosworth, seeing her smile. She had not been asking about his cousin because of any interest in him, then but rather because she had been thinking about him in terms of the lost ring.

"My father's ring?"

Miss Bosworth nodded.

"Yes."

With a shake of his head, Henry shrugged.

"I do not think so. He was not in London when my ring was taken for the first time and–"

"That you are aware of."

A frown wrapped itself around Henry's forehead.

"What do you mean?"

"Simply that," Miss Bosworth continued, nonchalantly. "If your cousin had not introduced himself to you, would you have known who he was? Would you have recognized him?"

Slowly, Henry began to realize what she meant... and the thought was a troubling one.

"No, I do not think I would have done."

"Then is there not even the smallest chance that your cousin could have taken the ring? I do not say such things to lay the blame at his feet, but simply because it must surely be a consideration!"

Henry thought on this for some moments before he replied. Time and again, he looked at Miss Bosworth, worrying that she found his silence concerning, but she merely smiled at him whenever he caught her attention. Letting the idea play through his thoughts, trying to understand it all, he considered carefully.

"It would be foolish of me to suggest that there was no chance of my cousin being involved in this affair, certainly." Speaking slowly, he nodded, but kept his gaze to the path now. "Though my inclination is to say that it could not be him."

"Which I quite understand. But it is only right to consider that he might be the one involved in this affair, before discounting that possibility out of hand." Miss Bosworth's hand tightened on his arm for a moment. "What would his purpose be in taking it, it if *is* he who is the guilty party?"

Considering this, Henry's frown quickly returned.

"It has my father's crest on it, though it is not the one that I use for my correspondence and the like. I had a new one made."

"Which bears a similarity to the old one?"

"A great deal of similarity," Henry agreed, chewing on the edge of his lip.

"I see." Miss Bosworth's murmur sent a coldness running through Henry's frame as he understood now what Miss Bosworth meant by suggesting such a thing. If the crest was similar, then his cousin might take his father's crest and use it for his gain – or, at the very least, attempt to do so.

"Though my cousin, as I have said, is a good fellow. He is a hard-working sort, who has removed his name and his family from whatever difficulties his father had left them in. I would be surprised if he went to such lengths to cheat me out of such a thing as my fortune."

Miss Bosworth smiled up at him, though her eyes were a little sorrowful.

"I suppose it would depend on how deep or difficult such circumstances were. If he believes that he was treated unfairly in some way, then he might be more than willing to take the crest from you."

Henry shook his head.

"I should not like to think of it."

"Then we will not." Miss Bosworth tossed her head, her

red curls bouncing. "Then who else might have done such a thing?" A moment or two of silence passed before she looked up at him again. "Might Lady Judith be involved?"

Surprise rippled through him.

"Lady Judith? I did not know you were acquainted with her."

"I was not – I *have* not been formally introduced – but she spoke to me last evening, demanding to know first of all why Miss Fairley and I were out walking together and secondly, what it was you and I had been speaking of." A sudden smile spread across her features, stealing away Henry's surprise. "I think she was the one you were attempting to escape from when we first met, was she not?"

Remembering what he had done, Henry chuckled and nodded.

"Yes, she was. I am not sorry for doing such a thing, though you might wish me to be."

"No, I certainly do not want you to regret it!" Laughing, Miss Bosworth leaned closer to him as the afternoon sun danced across the dappled leaves above them. "I enjoyed our waltz and, knowing now that our acquaintance has grown from such a meeting, makes my heart all the happier."

Henry smiled back at her, aware of all that his heart was trying to say, but struggling to bring such words to his lips.

"I would quite agree."

It was a far cry from what he wanted to express to her, but Miss Bosworth's warm smile told him that she was grateful for what he *had* said.

"I do not think that Lady Judith would agree, however," she continued, making him laugh aloud. "Though, is there any reason for *her* to steal your ring?"

Quietening, Henry let himself consider it before he

gave her his answer. It did not take as much thought as it had done for his first cousin, and Henry quickly shook his head.

"I am not very well acquainted with the lady – although I will say that she is my second cousin – so there could be no easy way for her to know of my talisman ring and how much it was worth," he said, as Miss Bosworth's lips flattened, her thoughts clearly rushing one over the other. "While I knew her name, I was not introduced to her until this Season. My father and her mother are cousins, but their family was not known to us."

"She clearly has an interest in you."

"Perhaps." Henry smiled and shrugged one shoulder. "But I am afraid that I have no particular interest in her."

Miss Bosworth's cheeks flushed red, but she kept her gaze to his, their steps slowing as they continued to meander. Henry did not know what to say, his thoughts no longer fixed on his cousin, Lady Judith, or his talisman ring, but instead focused entirely on Miss Bosworth. She was everything he could have hoped for in a young lady, albeit a little more outspoken than he might have preferred. With a beauty all of her own, and a strength which had helped her with her standing in society thus far, he both admired and respected her – and that was not something he felt with such strength for any other young lady of his acquaintance.

"Is there anyone else you might think of?" Miss Bosworth's voice had become a little quieter now, her gaze tugging away from his. "Any other young lady or gentleman of your acquaintance? Anyone eager for your company, even though you might be less than inclined?"

Attempting to think of those he had engaged with of late, instead of letting his thoughts focus on Miss Bosworth, Henry let out a sigh and shook his head.

"I cannot say. There was only one other young lady I considered at one moment, but it did not last for too long."

"Oh?"

"A Miss Blakefield." His shoulders rounded as a stab of pain pushed itself into his heart. "She suggested that I might have had a little happiness on the day that my father passed away since I was now to take the title."

"Good gracious!"

Henry looked at her, seeing the way her eyes had rounded, the shock flaring through them, and felt his heart swell with affection for her all the more.

"Indeed."

"I am sorry to hear that." Miss Bosworth put her other hand on his arm, turning herself towards him a little more. "It must have brought a great shock to you to hear her say such a thing."

"I could not imagine being wed to a lady who cared only for the title, and what it might bring her." Henry shook his head, looking into Miss Bosworth's eyes and knowing in his heart that she would never say such a thing to him. "I did not rejoice for a single moment over the loss of my father. My grief was, in fact, so painful that I did not think I would ever be able to find even the smallest relief from it. I would say, if I was truthful, that it has *not* left me, but continues to linger, though I have just become a little more used to its presence."

Miss Bosworth nodded slowly.

"I recall the loss of my grandmother." There was a quietness to her voice now which, no doubt, came from grief. It was a quietness which Henry understood, for it climbed into his soul also, whenever he spoke of his late father. "She was very dear to me and, given that I am the youngest of my sisters, I was able to spend more time in her company than they, given that they had to begin their education and refinements. I recall sitting beside her as she read aloud and thinking her voice to be the most soothing in all the world."

"It is a pain you understand, then."

She looked up at him again.

"Yes, though not in the same way. My father is very much alive – heartily so!"

That made Henry smile.

"Does he have an heir? You have never spoken of a brother."

Miss Bosworth winced.

"Yes, I have a brother. He is the very eldest of us all, by some years. He is already married."

"And then only daughters?"

A smile spread across her face as she looked up at him, her eyes twinkling.

"I believe that my father was hoping that a 'spare' would be produced eventually, but alas, I was the very last child to be born to my father and I, unfortunately, was a daughter also. Four daughters were more than enough, I am sure."

Henry chuckled at that, enjoying the company of Miss Bosworth immensely.

"I must say, I think that–"

"Good afternoon, Lord Yarmouth."

Stopping abruptly, Henry realized, a little too late, that, in coming around the corner, they had come to a small group of gentlemen and ladies, all of whom were looking at himself and Miss Bosworth walking arm in arm. It was not to them that he looked, however, but to the grinning face of Lord Falconer, who was clearly delighted to see them out together.

"Good afternoon, Falconer. Do excuse us, we had no intention of interrupting your conversation."

"And yet, you have done so – and I welcome it, as I am sure we all do." Turning, Lord Falconer put his arm wide. "You will already be acquainted with Lord Symington, Miss Blakefield, Miss Marton, and Lord Stepps, yes?"

"Yes, of course."

Glancing at Miss Bosworth and seeing her light frown as she curtsied, Henry quickly made the introductions, silently hoping that Miss Bosworth would not be too put out to have to stop and converse for a few minutes. As much as he glowered at Lord Falconer, however, his friend barely gave him a second of notice and instead began talking of the recent enjoyments of London.

"I do wonder at you walking out in the afternoon sunshine, Lord Yarmouth."

Henry blinked, a little surprised at the interruption, which had nothing to do with the conversation at hand.

"Is that so, Miss Blakefield? Why should you be surprised? It is a fine day, and the sun is warm. I should think it–"

"No parasol, Miss Bosworth?" Miss Blakefield interrupted again, turning sharp eyes upon the lady as Henry felt her stiffen. "I am surprised. Wallflowers must be very careful in the sunshine, given that they spend so much time in the dark shadows. To be outside on such a fine day must surely be a little overwhelming."

Miss Bosworth sniffed.

"Not in the least."

Her eyes fastened to his and Henry offered a small smile of encouragement, wondering if there was more that she wished to say, but was holding herself back from it. If she were doing so, then he appreciated her valiant effort more than he could express.

"*That* is why I am surprised to see you out walking, Lord Yarmouth," Miss Blakefield continued, turning her attention to Henry again. "There is *many* a young lady for you to be walking with. You need not waste your time on wallflowers, given that they will never come to anything." She lifted her chin, her eyes darting back to Miss Bosworth. "They are *meant* to fade away, not to be brought out to parade their dwindling beauty for a short while. It only prolongs their state and is much more of a punishment than might otherwise be expected, I am sure."

The shock of her coldness towards Miss Bosworth – for speaking of her indirectly was poor form in itself – stunned Henry into silence. Indeed, the entire group said nothing and all that could be heard was the whisper of the wind in the trees and the gentle calling of the birds within them.

And then, Miss Bosworth spoke.

"I think you will find, Miss Blakefield, that Lord Yarmouth is not a gentleman who is easily swayed by what society dictates. He is a gentleman who knows his own mind, who can *think* on matters, rather than being swayed to one course of action simply because everyone else is doing that thing." She smiled tightly, though her tone remained level. Henry smiled, but not because the lady was speaking so highly of him and, in doing so, making it quite plain that Miss Blakefield, to her mind, was narrow-minded, but because he was rather delighted by the confidence with which the lady spoke. She was not about to allow Miss Blakefield to embarrass her. Many other young ladies might have turned away in mortification, but not Miss Bosworth. Instead, she was courageous and determined and Miss Blakefield would end up the one ashamed. "I think such traits are to be admired, do you not? To be able to think for oneself, to allow one's own thoughts to take the place of societal expectation and influence is an incredible gift – and a very rare thing, I think. Lord Yarmouth should be admired, Miss Blakefield, not rebuked. Unless it is that you cannot see what is plain for someone such as myself to see about his character?"

Noting the way that Miss Blakefield's cheeks warmed, Henry kept the smile off his face with a great deal of effort, making certain not to permit even a single flicker to touch the edge of his mouth. He looked at Miss Blakefield with a slightly lifted eyebrow, waiting for her to respond, but the lady's lips were flat, held into a thin line as the rest of the group looked at her also.

No one was looking at Miss Bosworth, Henry noticed. Every eye was upon Miss Blakefield, waiting for her to respond, waiting for her to say something in response to Miss Bosworth's question, but the longer the silence grew, the more it seemed as though she could not find a single thing to say.

"I think that I quite agree with you there, Miss Bosworth."

Lord Stepps, clearly unable to bear the silence any longer, turned with a smile to Miss Bosworth and Henry let out a slow breath, still watching Miss Blakefield out of the corner of his eye. She was now red in the face, her arms folded across her chest and, as Miss Bosworth and Lord Stepps fell into conversation, Miss Blakefield stamped her foot, turned sharply, and strode away – swiftly followed by her lady's maid who had been standing a short distance away.

Henry smiled to himself, only to catch Lord Falconer's eye. His friend was grinning, one eyebrow arching in

Henry's direction and, try as he might, Henry could not help but grin right back. The way that Miss Bosworth had spoken of him had given his spirits a lift, his heart renewed in its dedication to the lady. The more time that he spent with her, the more time he *wished* to spend with her, and as Henry turned his gaze to Miss Bosworth once more, he found himself with a certainty in his soul which he had never had before.

If she would agree, then he would ask Miss Bosworth to accept his court. He had no desire to tarry, no eagerness to wait a little longer, to take tea and take another walk thereafter; no, he wanted to move their connection further than before – and he wanted to do so without the smallest bit of delay.

CHAPTER FIFTEEN

"Are you truly attempting to make enemies of everyone we are acquainted with?" Joy blinked, turning her head just in time to see her mother storming into the room, a flush growing into her face as Lady Halifax continued to rail at her, clearly unaware that Joy had company. "I have only just now heard from one of my friends that you spoke in a *very* rude fashion to another young lady!" Lady Halifax threw up her hands, her face now as red as Joy's. "You insulted her, suggested that she was slow in her thinking or some such thing. Why must you do such a thing as that, Joy? Have you no interest in furthering your connections in society? You have already ruined your chances for a match almost entirely, and still, you do not learn? What else is there that must happen to you? What other consequences must your sharp tongue face, before you realize what it is that you are doing? You are already a wallflower. Do you want to be spurned by society altogether?" Shaking her head, Lady Halifax sighed aloud and shook her head. "I think that mayhap, we should return home. Your father is disappointed enough already with all that I have told him in my letters. I am sorry that I shall have to write of yet more foolishness on your part."

"Mama."

Joy lifted her eyebrows, widening her eyes, but her mother was clearly in great distress and continued speaking regardless, ignoring her.

"I have had to endure more than enough, Joy." Lady Halifax flung her hands up again and then let them fall to her sides. "It is time to return home."

"That would be a great shame."

Much to Joy's mortification, her mother let out a small shriek of surprise, her eyes flaring wide as she stared at Lord Yarmouth who had come to call only a few minutes before Lady Halifax had arrived. Having sent the maid for her mother – though another remained in the room for propriety's sake – Joy had expected her mother to come in with a warm smile and, perhaps, a little curiosity. She had not expected to be spoken to in such a cold fashion, and to have had her do so in front of Lord Yarmouth was all the more of an embarrassment.

"Lord... Lord...?"

"Lord Yarmouth, Mama." Quickly getting to her feet, Joy came a little closer to her mother and, with great firmness, grasped her arm and then led her to a comfortable chair. "I did send the maid to fetch you. Lord Yarmouth has come to call on me."

"To call on you?" Lady Halifax repeated, turning to look at Joy with such wide eyes, that it was as though she could not quite believe that such a thing had taken place. "I... I see."

Lord Yarmouth rose to his feet and bowed, just as Lady Halifax collapsed back into her chair.

"I am very glad to see you again, Lady Halifax. Though

I must say, I do hope that your return home might be reconsidered? I had every intention of spending as much time as possible in Miss Bosworth's company, which I cannot do should she return home!"

Lady Halifax blinked rapidly, her color changing so quickly from red to puce that Joy wondered if she might have to send for the smelling salts! Glancing at Lord Yarmouth, she quickly hid a smile, seeing the twinkle in his eye. Apparently, the thought that someone might come to call on Joy was almost too much to take in for her mother!

"I have sent for tea, Mama. It will be here presently." Turning to Lord Yarmouth, Joy merely spread her hands by way of apology, only for Lord Yarmouth to chuckle softly. "I think your presence may have stayed my return home," Joy whispered, as her mother began to fan herself with one hand before sending off the maid to fetch her fan. "Thank you for that."

"I do mean every word of what I said," came the quiet reply. "I should like to be in your company as much as I can."

Joy's eyes widened as a kick of excitement to her stomach sent her heart pounding.

"Truly? Even though I am a wallflower who speaks much too sharply to others?"

Lord Yarmouth grinned.

"I do not think you did anything wrong as regards Miss Blakefield – and I shall say that to your mother! But yes, I should very much like to court you, Miss Bosworth. That was my intention in coming here today, though I had hoped to speak to your mother of the idea before asking you, but I am not certain that she would be able to even listen to me at the present moment!" His eyes searched her face. "What would you say if I were to ask you, Miss Bosworth? Would you accept me?"

"Of course I would."

It was rarely that Joy was embarrassed by how quickly she spoke but, on this occasion, her eagerness had displayed itself with such earnestness that she could not help but flush. Thankfully, Lord Yarmouth only smiled, his eyes twinkling as she dropped her head and then turned her attention back to her mother, waiting until her embarrassment faded a little before she looked back at Lord Yarmouth.

Inside, however, her heart was leaping about in such a frenzy that it was difficult to even take a breath. Her whole body was sparking, tingling in her fingertips and her toes.

Lord Yarmouth wishes to court me!

The joy of it was not something she could even think to explain, and she closed her eyes as the tea tray was brought in, using the distraction of it to quieten herself as best she could, squeezing her hands into tight fists so that she might be able simply to draw breath.

"I should like to say, Lady Halifax, that I was present during the conversation between your daughter, myself, and Miss Blakefield." Joy's eyes flew open as Lord Yarmouth spoke, looking first at him and then back to her mother, who was still staring at Lord Yarmouth as though she expected him to vanish at any time. "I do not know who has told you that your daughter was the one at fault, but I can assure you that every word which was said was more than fair," Lord Yarmouth continued, as Joy rose, thinking to pour the tea rather than stare at Lord Yarmouth as he spoke. Her hands trembled a little as she picked up the teapot, realizing that, for the first time, someone was coming to the defense of her behavior rather than choosing to rail at her for it.

It was a most unusual feeling – and one which Joy was not at all used to. It warmed through her and as she poured the tea carefully, a soft smile spread across her face. Lord Yarmouth thought that she had behaved well, that she had spoken clearly and without malice. He was coming to protect her, to stand against whatever rumors had been whispered about her. It was truly a wonderful sensation.

"Is that so?" Lady Halifax shifted a little in her seat, her eyes darting to Joy and then back to Lord Yarmouth again. "I am a little surprised to hear that. My daughter is not known for her good judgment."

The teapot trembled a little more in Joy's hands, but she poured the tea steadily and kept her eyes fixed on it rather than look at either her mother or Lord Yarmouth. To hear her mother say such things was not unexpected, but it was painful. Did she truly think so little of her?

"And I am surprised to hear *you* say such a thing," Lord Yarmouth replied, with a firmness that surprised Joy. "I have always found Miss Bosworth considered and careful." Smiling, he turned his head and looked at her. "To be frank, Lady Halifax, given what Miss Blakefield said and the insults she threw at your daughter, I found myself quite in awe of the restraint with which she returned those remarks."

Lady Halifax frowned.

"Do you mean to say that Miss Blakefield insulted Joy in some way?"

Joy served the tea to her mother and managed not to roll her eyes in her mother's direction as she did. She had not spoken of what had taken place with Miss Blakefield for she had considered that there was no reason for her to do so, not when she had fully expected her mother to neither listen nor care. It was only because Lord Yarmouth was speaking of it that Lady Halifax was willing to listen.

"Miss Blakefield suggested that I ought not to give your daughter much of my time – if any at all," Lord Yarmouth stated, shaking his head as Lady Halifax took in a breath. "I was horrified to hear her speak so unkindly. To my mind, Lady Halifax, your daughter ought never to have even *been* a wallflower! I have heard of what took place with Lord Dartford and I can assure you, I would have said the same thing to him in return, had he been speaking to me. How could he be so insulting to not only your daughter but also to your elder daughters?"

Lady Halifax blinked.

"What do you mean?"

"To say aloud that none of your elder daughters had ever caught his interest and that now, he believed that Miss Bosworth would be unable to do so either, is *most* uncouth. I am surprised that so many people within the *ton* believe it is acceptable. It seems very unfair to my mind that the *ton* are willing to push your daughter back, simply for defending herself, and her sisters, while permitting all that Lord Dartford says to pass by without incident. I am sure that you will agree."

Joy took the teacup to Lord Yarmouth and smiled at him as she did so, seeing his eyes flick towards her mother and then back up to her. The gratitude in her heart was so heavy, she could not even think of how to express it, save for catching his hand in one of hers for a brief moment as, with the other, she set the tea down in front of him.

Lord Yarmouth's eyes met hers again, and this time, he smiled softly as his fingers pressed hers. And then the moment was gone, and Joy was forced to sit back down again, away from him but the warmth of his touch lingered still.

"That is a perspective which I have not seen the incident from before." Lady Halifax took a sip of her tea and then set it back down, looking at Lord Yarmouth as though he were a complete stranger who had only just set foot into the townhouse. "Are you quite certain that you were present with my daughter when Miss Blakefield spoke as she did?"

"Yes, I am quite certain." Lord Yarmouth dropped his head for a moment, clearly hiding his smile before looking back at the lady. "As were my dear friend, Lord Falconer, and several others. Lord Falconer will certainly verify what I have said if that is what you wish?"

From the way that her mother's eyes darted to Joy and then back again, Joy knew at once that this was precisely what her mother wished to do, but Lady Halifax only laughed and then shook her head.

"No, of course not. Your word is enough. Well, I shall speak to this Miss Blakefield and demand to know exactly what it was she meant by stating that my daughter ought not to be in your company, Lord Yarmouth." A slightly triumphant smile spread across her face as Joy's eyes rounded, a little surprised to hear her mother speak so. "And the *ton* will learn that I am not about to push my daughter forward to take the blame for something she did not do."

She thought to herself that this was *not* the time to ask her mother why she had not done such a thing before now, or to demand to know why she had not even so much as spoken to her before deciding that the *ton* were in the right about what had been said about her as regarded Miss Blakefield, Joy chose to stay silent and merely smile at Lord Yarmouth who had not, perhaps, realized just how much he had done in coming to defend her. His small smile back at her made her heart swell, and she took a deep breath, sitting a little taller now.

Perhaps her mother would not continually berate her, or even consider her a wallflower for much longer, given the way that she was speaking to Lord Yarmouth. The kind way that he had spoken of her, the sweetness with which his words had come about, meant a great deal – more than she could express – and suddenly, her hopes for the remainder of the Season drew themselves up, big and bright.

Perhaps she would find happiness yet.

CHAPTER SIXTEEN

*W*ith a broad smile still on his face, Henry walked into his townhouse, only to be met by a hubbub of activity. Footmen and maids were scurrying about, and his butler was nowhere to be seen. No one came to take his hat and gloves and, when he finally caught someone's attention, the footman's eyes were wide with alarm and Henry noticed how the man's hands trembled.

"What has happened?" he asked, not raising his voice for fear of upsetting the man even more. "Where is the butler?"

"I don't know what happened, my Lord." The footman shook his head. "The butler was found on the study floor."

Henry blinked in surprise, snatching in a breath.

"I beg your pardon?"

"The butler. I don't know if he was showing someone into your study, but someone clearly hit him from behind. There's a swelling here." Indicating the center of the back of his head, the footman winced. "The other men have taken him to his rooms and the housekeeper sent for the physician, who arrived a short while ago. She said that you would want him to have the physician."

"Yes, of course!" A little astonished, Henry rubbed one hand over his eyes. "You say he was hit on the head? By whom? Who came to call?"

"I don't know, my Lord." The footman shook his head, his face white. "There was a lot of blood. The maids are cleaning it now. I just hope that he's going to be all right."

It did not make any sense whatsoever. Why would someone walk into his study and hit the butler?

Unless they were doing so simply to have unbound access to my things.

His eyes closed.

"Was anything taken?"

The footman looked blankly back at him until Henry was forced to repeat the question, only for the man to nod.

"That is to say, I am not sure what was taken, my Lord, only that something must have been, given the state of the room."

"The state of the room?" Henry repeated, as the footman nodded fervently. "I do not understand."

The footman looked down the hallway, one hand out towards it.

"Might you go and see for yourself, my Lord. Your eyes will do a better job than any of my attempts at explaining."

Henry nodded and stepped away, leaving the footman to take his hat and gloves to their usual place. With a heart beginning to beat furiously in his chest, he began to make his way to the study, only for a familiar voice to call his name.

"Yarmouth? What has happened here? I saw the physician arriving and thought –"

"Falconer." Henry closed his eyes and shook his head as

his friend came in. "I am quite well. The physician did not come for me."

"There is a small crowd outside," Lord Falconer told him, settling one hand on Henry's shoulder and peering into his face as if to make quite certain that he was well. "What has happened?"

Turning back, Henry gestured to his study and began to walk again.

"My butler has been hit on the back of the head and left to linger in unconsciousness and pain. Blood is on the floor and the footman told me that it would be best if I saw the room for myself, rather than have him explain it."

"Good gracious." Falling into step with him, Lord Falconer came into the study with Henry, his eyes rounding in much the same way that Henry's did. "Someone was looking for something."

Henry let his eyes flicker across the room, never lingering on any one thing, but taking in the mess and the disarray without fear or hesitation. He wanted to see it all just as it was, to try to make sense of what had happened, but the shock was a little too great.

"Do you know what it could be?" Lord Falconer asked, leaning a little closer to Henry now, to avoid having all of Henry's staff hear what he was saying. "What this person – whoever it was – was searching for?"

Shaking his head, Henry let out a slow breath and pinched the bridge of his nose.

"I cannot imagine. And the only person who can tell me who was present is the butler who is, at this very moment, is unconscious and being seen by the physician."

Running one hand over his face, Henry let out a slow breath and tried to keep the panic from kicking back at him. Whoever had been in here, whoever had been rifling through his things, had been searching for something and Henry did not know whether they had managed to find it. In his mind's eye, he suddenly saw a vision of Miss Bosworth – not because he blamed her in any way, but because Henry knew how much he valued her companionship, her support, and her thoughts on something like this.

The ring.

Heaving in a breath, Henry tore across the room and attempted to drag open the drawer of his study desk. Much to his relief, it was still locked.

"They were not able to find what they were looking for because I had locked the desk drawer," he explained, as Lord Falconer's eyebrows lifted. "It must be the talisman ring."

Lord Falconer let out a hiss of breath through his teeth.

"Do you think so?"

"What other explanation could there be?"

Pulling the key from his pocket, Henry unlocked the drawer and, opening it, lifted the ring from the small box in which it had been contained, and then held it high.

"You have it?"

"I have it." Relief ran in rivulets over his skin and despite everything that had taken place, he smiled briefly. "I have no intention of permitting this to be taken from my sight or my person again."

"What will you do with it?"

Henry turned the ring over in his hand and then placed it on his finger.

"I will find a chain and place it around my neck," he said, decisively. "If this is truly what was being sought then I will not take that risk again."

Lord Falconer nodded and then looked around the room.

"You think that whoever did this would try again?"

"I do not know if they would dare, especially not now that the butler knows who it is... though he cannot tell us as yet." Henry scowled and looked back at his friend. "I think that I must go to see how he fares."

"I will come with you." Lord Falconer's frown was heavy, his eyes dark with concern. "This is not good, Yarmouth. This is not good at all."

Henry sighed and lifted his shoulders.

"I am well aware of that, Falconer. But what can I do?"

His friend said nothing, his gaze drifting around the room as Henry took it in for the second time, feeling still rather stunned about what had happened to his house. A shudder ran down his spine and he shivered visibly, his eyes closing as he considered all that had happened in his absence. This had taken a great deal of boldness on someone's part and showed almost a desperation in their actions. They had waited until he had gone from the house and, thereafter, sought to find the one thing which Henry possessed that they wanted.

And if it was the ring, then what reason would there be for them to do such a thing as this? What was it that possession of the ring held for them, promised to them, that they would be willing to go to such an extreme course of action to get it?

Looking down at it, Henry waited for the answer to come, but nothing was there, except more questions.

I will need to tell Miss Bosworth.

A little surprised at how much his heart yearned for her, how much he wished that she was standing here with him, Henry closed his eyes and drew in a breath to steady himself before opening his eyes again and going to the door. While his staff could tidy up the room for him, he had a responsibility to them, which meant going to see his butler and making certain that the very best care was given to the man.

The rest of it could come after that.

"He has regained consciousness."

Henry blew out a breath of relief.

"That is good."

"But he can remember nothing," the physician continued, as Henry frowned. "He does not know who was at the door, what happened to him, or even what day of the week it is! These things are common when there has been an accident involving the head."

All hope of finding out who it was that had come into his house and injured his butler ran from Henry's mind and he lowered his head, running one hand through his hair.

"I see."

"It may return," the physician finished, putting one hand on Henry's arm for a moment. "But it may not. It is hard to tell in such situations as these."

"And what needs to happen?" Henry looked at him carefully. "He must rest for some days, I imagine?"

The physician nodded.

"The cut has been stitched and bandaged, and I will come back to check on it in three days. Yes, he must rest and recover from the shock, and from his injuries, and if were you, I would offer him a little brandy in the evenings especially. I have left some laudanum for his pain and to help with sleep, but he has refused to take it, thus far."

"I will speak with him," Henry said, quickly. "Thank

you for attending him. Send me the account at once and I shall have it paid directly."

After promising that he would do so, the physician hurried away, and Henry turned back to the butler's bedchamber, seeing the man lying so very still on the bed, his eyes closed, and the blankets pulled up over his shoulders. A maid was sitting with him, and Henry had already obtained the housekeeper's promise that the butler would never be left alone until he was fully recovered. The urge to go to his bedside, to have him answer as many questions as he possibly could was strong, but Henry dampened it easily enough and turned around to walk back out of the room.

"I am sorry, my Lord."

The hoarse whisper had Henry turning around sharply, seeing one of the butler's hands lift limply.

"You have nothing to apologize for." Coming across the room to the butler's bedside, Henry settled one hand on the man's shoulder and smiled. "Rest. This was not of your doing, and I hold nothing against you."

The butler could barely find the strength to open his eyes.

"Thank you, my Lord."

"Rest now." Lifting his hand, Henry stepped back. "I do not hold you in the least responsible," he said again, as the butler's chest rose and fell, his eyes closing again. Watching the man drift into sleep, Henry sighed heavily and let his shoulders slump and his head drop forward. Whoever had done this had caused the butler a great injury, and Henry found himself growing angry at the sheer inconsideration that had been shown to the butler. Whoever had come into Henry's home had come intending to injure whoever stood in the way of whatever it was that they wished to get – and they had done precisely that.

I wish I had been at home so that I might have dealt with this perpetrator face to face.

"Cousin!"

Henry lifted his head, surprised to see none other than Mr. Brackwell hurrying down the servants' staircase.

"Brackwell. Whatever are you doing here?"

"I was coming to take my leave of you, but I came upon such a dreadful scene, I felt obliged to come and find you to make certain that all was well."

"All is *not* well." Henry shook his head again and then gestured for his cousin to climb back up the staircase. "Come. Did you say that you are taking your leave?"

"I am." Silence fell for a few minutes as they climbed the staircase back to the main part of the house. "My business is concluded and thus, I feel that it is time for me to return home."

"But what–"

Henry winced, only for his cousin to let out a wry laugh.

"What of Miss Bosworth? My dear cousin, I was to walk with her, was I not? But I realized shortly thereafter that the lady is only eager for *your* company and yours alone."

Henry pressed his lips tightly together to stop himself from smiling broadly.

"I am sorry."

"There is no need to be!" With a smile, Mr. Brackwell set one hand on Henry's shoulder. "I am glad for you and, given that I have made a good few acquaintances here in London – acquaintances who will be of benefit to me, given their expertise and knowledge in certain areas – I return home with a smile on my face and gladness in my heart."

"And the assurance, I hope, that you will soon find the right young lady to marry." With a chuckle, Henry rolled his eyes. "There is always Lady Judith, I suppose! She is both family *and* unattached!"

Much to Henry's surprise, his cousin did not smile at this. Instead, his brows dropped low over his eyes, and he tilted his head.

"Lady Judith?" he repeated, as Henry nodded, confused now as to why his cousin seemed so uncertain. "I do not think... no, that cannot be so. She is not unattached, as you might think her."

"Indeed?" With a laugh, Henry chased away his confusion. "Then I am glad. It means, mayhap, that she will not pursue me!"

Mr. Brackwell put one hand out, silencing Henry.

"You mean to say that you do not know that Lord Falconer and Lady Judith are attached? They are courting, I believe, although it is meant to be quite secret."

Henry's shoulders dropped, his smile fading.

"I beg your pardon?"

"You did not know?" Mr. Brackwell shrugged. "I do not like society gossip, and so I did not say anything but yes, they are courting, and she begged me to keep it a secret. She also barely acknowledged me which did frustrate me a great deal." A frown tugged at Mr. Brackwell's forehead. "It was not as though–"

"Wait a moment." Confused, Henry rubbed hard at his forehead, his eyes squeezing tightly closed. "You mean to say that our second cousin, Lady Judith, is being courted by Lord Falconer? How long has this been going on?"

"I do not know." Now it was Mr. Brackwell who looked confused. "Why do you ask? I did not think you had any feelings for the Lady!"

"I do not!" Henry exclaimed, quickly, dropping his hands. "It is all so very strange, for Lord Falconer teased me about the lady and then encouraged me towards her... only to then laugh when I realized that her character was not one which I would be drawn to. Why would he do such a thing if he was eager to court her? Why would he not tell me?"

Mr. Brackwell hesitated, then put out both hands.

"I do not know, but mayhap those are the wrong questions to be asking."

Henry's frown returned.

"What do you mean?"

"I mean that you need not ask why he would not tell you, or why he was courting her while pushing you towards her, for these questions will lead only to more confusion. There is one question, however, which must be answered which is, I think, a good deal more important than any of the others you have mentioned."

"Which is?"

Mr. Brackwell's hands fell back to his sides.

"What reason did he have in keeping this hidden from you?"

CHAPTER SEVENTEEN

"*V*iscount Yarmouth!"

Joy smiled indulgently at her mother.

"Yes, Mama. Viscount Yarmouth."

"That is most extraordinary," Lady Halifax continued, as she walked around the ballroom, arm in arm with Joy. "It seems that, even though you were pushed into becoming a wallflower, you are now to be quite happily married, should all go well!" Her eyes turned to Joy's, only for her smile to be wiped away. "But you must not do *anything* which will push him away from you, do you understand?"

"I have no intention of doing anything of the sort," Joy replied, firmly. "Though do not ask me to change my character in any way, for I will not even be willing to listen to such a suggestion."

Lady Halifax – much to Joy's surprise – laughed.

"I have no intention of doing anything of the sort, I assure you. It seems that my attempts to do so failed dramatically, and now you have managed to catch a Viscount simply by being as you are!" Her smile faded and she paused for a moment, her steps slowing. "Though I am sorry that I listened to the gossips, before I spoke to you about what had happened with Miss Blakefield. That was not right. I should not have done such a thing, and I apologize for doing so." Joy blinked, rather stunned by what her mother had said. It was the first time that she could remember her mother ever apologizing to her, and it was almost as though a huge gust of wind had knocked her clean off her feet. "There are many things I should have done – or chosen *not* to do - this Season," Lady Halifax continued, sadly. "I apologize for my lack of consideration. It seems, however, that you have done very well without me and for that, I am truly glad."

"Thank you, Mama."

To her even greater astonishment, her mother embraced her right there in the middle of the ballroom and then kissed her cheek before turning and walking again, as though everything was just as it ought to be. Still stunned, Joy felt herself being pulled along as she tried to take in all that had just happened, overwhelmed, and truly delighted at all that her mother had said.

"Oh, there are my friends." With a smile, she stopped and waved, looking at her mother. "Might I step away for a few minutes?"

"But of course."

With a smile, Joy left her mother's side and hurried to the other wallflowers, glad to see them standing away from the walls and in with the other guests.

"Good evening! I am glad to see you all."

"As we are you!" Miss Simmons smiled, tilting her head. "We have heard everything that has happened of late, and we are all eager to discuss it with you!"

Joy flushed and closed her eyes, laughing softly.

"If you mean about what I said to Miss Blakefield, then I confess that I am not in the least bit sorry for it."

This sent a ring of laughter around the group and Joy's smile grew all the bigger. Despite the struggles she had faced, despite the troubles and the difficulties of becoming a wallflower, she had found some true friends here and that was a blessing indeed.

"Tell us all about it," Lady Frederica giggled, coming a little closer. "And do not leave anything out."

With a laugh, Joy began, her heart filled with more happiness and contentment than she had felt in many a week and with a smile that never once seemed to fade.

"I THINK Lord Yarmouth is an excellent gentleman, especially if he was so willing to speak to your mother in your defense."

"Yes, I think so." Joy frowned, her gaze sliding away. "He is to attend the ball this evening, and sent me a note to say that he wished to speak to me, but as yet, I have not seen him."

Miss Fairley giggled, and Joy's frown lifted.

"Mayhap he wishes to ask you something of the greatest importance."

"To ask me?" Joy flushed and shook her head. "I do not think so. It is much too soon in our connection and—"

"All the same, what *would* you say if he asked you to marry him?"

The answer came in the form of a thrill lifting Joy's heart, and the smile which split her features. Miss Fairley giggled again, and Joy looked away, keeping her expression as hidden from her friend as she could, but it was much too late.

"I am glad." With a sigh, Miss Fairley looked out across the ballroom and Joy followed her gaze, aware that they had retreated a little to the side of the ballroom. "Would that I could find someone as kind and as considerate."

"I am sure that you shall."

Miss Fairley smiled but it did not last.

"I do not think we shall all be as fortunate as you. I am very glad that you have encouraged us to step out from the dark shadows but all the same, no gentleman has truly looked at me, as Lord Yarmouth looked at you."

Joy reached across and squeezed Miss Fairley's hand.

"Do not give up hope. It will happen in time, I am sure. I – good gracious!"

Both she and Miss Fairley came to a sudden stop as, directly in front of them – though a little hidden in an alcove, they saw none other than Lady Judith. She was laughing and from where they stood, Joy could spy an arm around Lady Judith's waist.

No doubt, it was a gentleman.

"She is taking quite the risk standing there like that." Miss Fairley turned quickly and faced Joy so that they would not both be staring. "Shall we move away?"

Joy nodded, her stomach twisting as worry for the lady in question began to run through her.

"I think that we should – though what if someone turns and sees her? Her reputation could be ruined!"

"Whereas, if we stay, then we might pretend to be chaperoning her?" The doubt in Miss Fairley's voice had Joy sighing, her shoulders dropping. "It is not our responsibility to make certain that her reputation stays pristine, though I do appreciate your consideration. It is hers and hers alone."

"You are right."

As she went to turn around, Joy gasped in shock as the gentleman in question stepped out of the alcove, pointing out with one hand towards the other guests. Taking Lady Judith's hand in his, he tugged her away, though thankfully it was back towards the center of the ballroom rather than further into the shadows. Having clamped one hand over her mouth to hide the sound of her astonishment, Joy quickly let her hand fall again, though her eyes remained fixed and staring.

"What is it?" Miss Fairley asked, urgently. "Has something happened? Have they been seen?"

"It is... it is Lord Falconer!"

"Lord Falconer?" Looking a little confused, Miss Fairley turned, only for her eyebrows to lift. "That is Lord Yarmouth's friend, is it not?"

"It is." Joy blinked and then rubbed one hand over her eyes, hardly able to take in what she had seen. "From what Lord Yarmouth said, the gentleman always laughed about Lady Judith's character and mocked him for his initial interest – so why would he now be doing such a thing as to wrap his arms around her?"

Miss Fairley shrugged, clearly having no real understanding of why Joy was so surprised.

"Mayhap he is more of a rogue than we think."

It was an explanation, Joy supposed, but all the same, there was something about the connection that confused her. Why would Lord Falconer have done such a thing to Lord Yarmouth, if he was courting the lady himself? It seemed very strange indeed.

What if... what if both he and Lady Judith sought the ring for themselves for some purpose?

The thought bit down hard, and Joy could not get it to

release. It was a strange consideration, for surely to do such a thing would mean that Lord Falconer was not the friend that Lord Yarmouth considered him to be, and that would be painful for Lord Yarmouth to even think!

I must be wrong. It is a foolish thought.

"Are you quite all right?" Miss Fairley touched Joy's hand and she jumped, pulled from her thoughts. "What is wrong?"

"I was only thinking... thinking that there might be–"

"Ah, there you are! I was hoping to see you this evening!" Lord Yarmouth tapped Joy on the shoulder, and she turned around, though she did not smile, so many were her thoughts. "Forgive me for my tardiness in greeting you, I was caught up in conversation with Lord Knoxbridge and, as I walked in search of you, I had something of a skirmish with Lady Judith! Something caught my foot and I almost fell directly into her!"

"Lady Judith?" Joy repeated, aware that she sounded a little foolish, but continuing regardless. "Just now? At this very moment?" Recalling how Lord Falconer had pointed out one hand in the direction of the guests, Joy's stomach dropped to the floor. "Lord Yarmouth, where is your father's ring?" Lord Yarmouth's smile fell away as Miss Fairley looked on, her gaze going from one to the next in clear confusion. "Is it on your person?" Joy persisted, taking a small step closer. "Did you take it with you this evening?"

"I – I did." Lord Yarmouth shrugged. "But it is quite safe, I assure you. After what happened yesterday, I have taken extra precautions."

"Yesterday?" Joy put one hand on his arm. "Is this what you wished to speak to me about?"

Lord Yarmouth nodded, his light green eyes fixing to hers.

"It is. I came home after calling on you, and found that my butler had been knocked on the head with some implement and that whoever had done such a thing had then rummaged through my study, seeking something out!"

Joy's heart slammed against her ribs.

"Was it your ring?"

"I believe so, for what else has been taken from me of late?" Lord Yarmouth shook his head and sighed. "Thankfully, my ring was in the locked drawer where I had kept it, but from that moment, as I told Lord Falconer, I intended to keep it on a chain around my neck. I will not permit–"

"Is it still there?" Taking another step closer to him, Joy narrowed her eyes, trying to see the small, slim chain on which the ring might be. "You are quite sure that it is there still?"

Lord Yarmouth nodded.

"Of course. I am certain that no one could have taken it from me. No one knows that I kept it there."

"Save for Lord Falconer," Joy said slowly, as Lord Yarmouth began to grope around his neck, his fingers clearly seeking the small chain on which the ring was kept. "You said that you told him of it?"

Lord Yarmouth looked at her.

"Yes, because he had hurried into the house after me."

Joy frowned.

"He was in your company at the time?"

Dropping his hands to his side, Lord Yarmouth shook his head.

"No, he came in shortly after, stating that he... he did not give any reason as to why he was near my townhouse. All he said was that there was a small crowd outside."

Watching him, Joy noticed the way that his eyes rounded and then squeezed tightly closed again. Was he beginning to think in the same way as she? Could he see what it was that she had been trying to suggest?

"But no, it could not be!" In a low, dull whisper, Lord Yarmouth looked down at her, shaking his head. "I–"

"Where is the ring, Lord Yarmouth?" Joy asked, quickly. "Is it still on your person?"

Lord Yarmouth stared at her blankly for a few seconds and then, again, began to run his fingers around his shirt collar, clearly in search of the chain on which was his ring.

Nothing was there.

"It is gone."

There was no surprise in his voice now, no astonishment widening his eyes. Instead, there was a sadness, a heaviness in his face which Joy could hardly bear to see.

"I am sorry."

Taking a moment, she let her hand find his and squeezed his fingers gently, seeing the sorrowful smile curve around his lips.

"I would never have thought, not even for a moment, that my friend was involved in this." Lord Yarmouth closed his eyes tightly and let out a hiss of breath, shaking his head again. "I cannot quite believe..."

"There must be a purpose behind it." Miss Fairley spoke up for what was the first time during Joy and Lord Yarmouth's exchange and they both looked to her at once. "What is the reason for the theft? Why have they been trying to steal it from you?"

Lord Yarmouth looked away, his lips pinched but, eventually, he simply shook his head.

"I do not know."

"It bears your father's crest, does it not?" Joy asked as Lord Yarmouth nodded. "Could it be that they require that, for some reason? Does Lady Judith-?"

"The only way to know for certain is to go in search of them, demand to know, and have my ring returned to me." Interrupting her, Lord Yarmouth suddenly stood tall, his eyes flashing across the room, his jaw tight as his fingers laced through hers. "I will not let them take advantage of me – and nor will I permit them to laugh at me for my foolishness in believing that my friendship with Lord Falconer was exactly as it seemed. Come, Miss Bosworth, if you would? I have a question I must ask my friend."

Joy nodded and with a look at Miss Fairley, stepped away with Lord Yarmouth. Miss Fairley joined them, much to Joy's relief, glad that her silent appeal had been heard and understood. Though Joy very much wished to go with Lord Yarmouth, it would be best to be accompanied by a friend so that she would not be seen in Lord Yarmouth's company alone. To have her reputation questioned after she had only just managed to improve things between herself and her mother would not be a good idea!

"There is Lady Judith."

At Miss Fairley's murmur, Joy stopped and pulled Lord Yarmouth back who, to her mind, had been walking with great purpose through the ballroom but without any real idea of where Lord Falconer was.

"There is Lady Judith," she murmured, nodding in the lady's direction. "She is talking with a gentleman and will soon step out to dance, I think."

"Then I should sign my name to her dance card," Lord Yarmouth replied, his chin lifting, and his eyes narrowed. "That way, I will be able to ask her–"

"I have an idea as to how we might go about this," Joy interrupted, silently thinking to herself that, given the expression on Lord Yarmouth's face, Lady Judith would be suspicious of him the very moment that he stepped closer.

"Recall that neither Lady Judith nor Lord Falconer is aware of your suspicions as yet. We must make certain that they continue to be unaware of it."

Lord Yarmouth frowned.

"What do you mean?"

Joy let his hand go and took a step back, letting her thoughts settle into her mind.

"I think that we should speak with Lord Falconer – though you will have to rid yourself of the anger in your expression – and state that you have discovered something. You must speak of the ring as though you still have it."

Lord Yarmouth's frown grew deeper still.

"But I do not."

"You will say," Joy continued, quickly, "that the one you were wearing this evening has been taken, much to your frustration, of course, for you were hoping to use it to find the culprit, but that at least you have not lost the *real* ring. No doubt one of them will ask what you mean, and you will say–"

"That I had paste jewelry?" Lord Yarmouth's frown lifted as he began to understand. "And that the real ring still sits in my study desk back in my townhouse?"

Joy smiled and nodded as Miss Fairley let out a low exclamation of understanding.

"State that you intend to linger here for a little while longer, and might take yourself to White's thereafter. I do not doubt that Lord Falconer will take himself to your town-house almost immediately."

"Because he wants the ring so badly that it cannot be only just out of his reach," Miss Fairley murmured, as Joy nodded. "And you will confront him there, Lord Yarmouth."

"And I will speak to Lady Judith the very moment that

Lord Falconer has taken his leave. You will have to go quickly after him, to reach your house only a few minutes after his arrival." Seeing Lord Yarmouth nod slowly, she tilted her head, watching his expression. "What say you?"

Lord Yarmouth looked back at her, caught her hand again, and then lifted it to his lips. The kiss he placed upon it sent tingles up her arm and made Joy's breath hitch.

"I think it a capital idea," he murmured, softly. "Thank you. Now." With a broad smile, he released her hand. "Shall we go and find Lord Falconer?"

"You go to him," Joy replied, turning her attention to Lady Judith again. "I will wait here and watch Lady Judith, ready to speak to her once I see Lord Falconer depart."

Lord Yarmouth nodded, his gaze holding hers for a long moment.

"I will return to you, once this matter is at an end," he promised, the warmth in his tone sending flurries of anticipation into Joy's frame. "Wait for me."

She smiled back at him, clasping her hands tightly together in front of her.

"I shall."

CHAPTER EIGHTEEN

"Well, it has happened again!"

Lord Falconer's frown was so real, his confusion appearing so apparent, Henry would have found it difficult to believe it was all entirely false, had he not known it to be so.

"What has happened?"

"The ring has been taken from me."

His friend immediately threw up his hands.

"How can that be?" he exclaimed, sounding so utterly astonished, Henry began to wonder if he might have made a mistake in thinking that he was responsible. "You were wearing it on a chain around your neck, were you not?"

"I was. But the chain itself was a little visible around the back of my neck, though I did not think that anyone would think anything of it."

Lord Falconer rolled his eyes.

"And yet someone has pulled the chain – and the ring, I presume – from you? When did you first become aware of it?"

"Only a few minutes ago." Henry sniffed and shrugged. "It matters not."

At this, Lord Falconer's eyes opened wide.

"I beg your pardon?"

"It is as I have said," Henry continued, still doing his best to appear as entirely nonchalant as he could. "It does not particularly matter."

There came a silence between them which Henry made no effort to fill. Instead, he only smiled.

"I do not understand." Lord Falconer tilted his head, a frown on his face. "You do not care that your father's talisman ring has been taken?"

"I would care, had it been genuine." Seeing his friend's mouth fall open, Henry chuckled, forcing the sound out of his mouth. "I told a few people about what I was doing this evening as regards the ring and the chain. However, rather than place my father's genuine ring on the chain, I placed the paste ring there instead."

Lord Falconer blinked rapidly, his eyes now fixed on Henry.

"You have a paste version of your father's ring?"

"I do."

"And how long have you had it?"

Henry shrugged.

"I have had it for many a year, though I did not like to wear it." With a small sigh, Henry looked away. "To be truthful, the ring is such a pale imitation of the genuine talisman ring that it was an embarrassment to me to wear it. Of course, to the untrained eye, it would look like the real ring, but I would know that it was not. In that regard, I do not care that the ring has been taken, though I confess that it is still frustrating."

There was nothing but silence as Lord Falconer looked

into Henry's face and said nothing. Henry shrugged and then smiled, though inwardly, his stomach was busy tying itself into lots of tiny little knots. Was his friend going to believe him? Or would he realize that Henry had learned the truth about him?

"Goodness, what a disappointment that will be for whoever has taken your ring!" Lord Falconer cleared his throat gruffly and looked away, though Henry took in the little red dots in his friend's cheeks. "That is good, however. Good that you have not lost it."

"Yes, it is." Letting out what he hoped was a self-satisfied sigh, Henry grinned broadly. "The real ring is still in my study desk, though it is in a drawer which I have locked to be quite safe. I think that, once I return home, I will have it placed in the safe!"

Lord Falconer nodded.

"It sounds like a good idea." Clearing his throat for the second time, he looked around the room and shrugged. "I do not know if I will stay at this ball for much longer. I confess that I am a little bored."

"To White's, then?"

His friend shrugged.

"Mayhap. Do you intend to stay here a little longer?"

"I think so. I have some dances to enjoy, and Miss Bosworth is here also, so I am more than contented!"

Lord Falconer chuckled, though his eyes did not light up in their usual way.

"Very good. I shall let you return to her, then. If I do not see you again this evening, do let me know how things progress between yourself and Miss Bosworth." His eyebrows wiggled as he grinned, reminding Henry of just how good a friend Lord Falconer had been to him for so many years. "I can see that you are eager to further your acquaintance so, if anything significant should take place, then...?"

"Then I will inform you just as soon as I can, of course."

Unable to keep himself from smiling, Henry waved Lord Falconer away and then turned around himself, letting the smile slip from his face. Was his friend truly so good an actor as to be able to do such a thing as this? Had he truly been able to pretend for so long? Closing his eyes, Henry rubbed one hand over his face and then took a breath. He had to put such questions to one side and focus on regaining his father's talisman ring – and that meant following Lord Falconer from a distance. Turning back, he began to search for his friend, only to see him a short distance away, talking to none other than Lady Judith.

His heart shattered.

There had been within him the faint hope that what Mr. Brackwell had said about Lord Falconer was wrong, that his friend would *not* prove to be the thief, but now, seeing how Lord Falconer spoke in earnest to Lady Judith, his head lowering and his lips moving rapidly, Henry was sure that he had all of the proof that he needed. When his friend gestured towards the door, with Lady Judith nodding, one lip caught between her teeth, Henry followed Lord Falconer with his eyes as he stepped away.

It did not take him long to make his way out of the room and Henry followed close behind, dread in every step.

The time to end this was at the threshold – but how much would come tumbling down with it?

"THE NEXT TIME you decide to step into someone's house without invitation, I would appreciate it if you would choose not to injure their butler." Lord Falconer whipped around, his eyes wide and staring as Henry walked into the study, three footmen behind him barring the door. "I did not want to believe that you were the one who was involved in trying to take the ring from me," Henry continued, quietly. "But it seems as though Miss Bosworth is correct after all, and *I* am the one who has been a fool."

"I... I..."

There was nothing else for Lord Falconer to say. He had been found standing in Henry's study, a place he had not been invited into, with his hand at the drawer where Henry had told him that he kept the talisman ring.

"I do not understand." Henry's throat began to ache, his hands curling into fists as he glared at his friend, dampening down his anger as best he could. "Why would you do such a thing? Why would you try to steal from me?"

Lord Falconer swallowed, then stepped back from the desk, his hands lifted as though to show that he had done nothing wrong.

"I – I did not."

"You did. You and Lady Judith are, together, seeking the talisman ring of my father. Why would you take it?"

"She... she asked me to." Lord Falconer closed his eyes. "Lady Judith knows that I wish to marry her, but we cannot wed because I do not have a sufficient fortune."

"A sufficient fortune?" Henry repeated, not moving an inch from where he stood. "What are you talking about? You have an excellent fortune."

"Not enough to satisfy Lord Eltringham." Lord Falconer's jaw jutted forward. "And I may have been a little less economical than I ought to have been of late."

"And so, you thought that you would take my ring for its

monetary value?" Confused, Henry threw out his hands. "You know that it is worth very little!"

When Lord Falconer shook his head and then dropped it to his chest, Henry realized that there was more to the ring than he had first thought.

"You want it for the crest?" Speaking slowly, his eyes widened when his friend nodded. "You wish to use my ring to steal some of my wealth for your own gains?"

Lord Falconer threw his head back and groaned... and that was answer enough. Henry felt himself crumple inside, his heart heavy as he realized that the person whom he had called a friend for so many years was not his true friend at all. He was a man willing to do whatever he had to, to gain what *he* wanted. This was a man willing to steal, to injure, and to lie, so that he might find satisfaction in life, regardless of the detriment it might cause others. This was no gentleman, no kindhearted, friendly sort, as Henry had long believed. Instead, this was a man of whom Henry knew nothing. Dark-hearted, selfish, and entirely without consideration, he was a gentleman who thought only of himself.

"Lady Judith has an *excellent* dowry," Lord Falconer said, as though somehow that might excuse him for what he had done. "I must have it. It is the only way that I can pull myself from my current difficulties."

Henry closed his eyes. Every word made the pain – and his anger – grow.

"Why would you even let me *consider* her if you were already courting?"

Lord Falconer shrugged.

"It is not as though I care for her, Yarmouth. Surely you can see that! Why would I care for a young lady such as her, whose character I find so disagreeable?"

The anger that had been slowly building in Henry's

chest now blew into a great furnace, and he gritted his teeth together as Lord Falconer continued, waving a hand in Henry's direction as though all that he had said, all that he had done, was nothing more than a trifle.

"She is a means to an end," he continued, blithely. "I wanted to keep our arrangement as quiet as I could, until I made certain that my fortune was at the required standard for Lady Judith's father. Lady Judith agreed with me that we ought to do that. Thereafter, once I had her dowry – and whatever she is given each year by her father – I would, of course, have returned what I had borrowed to you. It all came about very quickly."

"I do not believe you."

Lord Falconer lifted an eyebrow.

"Why not?"

"Because had you had any honesty in this, had you shown even the smallest bit of integrity, then you would have come to talk to me about all of this first," Henry returned, taking a few steps closer to Lord Falconer. "You would have asked to borrow the money from me, rather than trying to steal it." His friend opened his mouth and then snapped it shut again, looking away. "Instead, you used me in the same way that you are trying to use Lady Judith," Henry continued, fire burning in the pit of his stomach. "You tell her that you care for her, that you want to marry her, but if she were to know the truth, she would discover that you care not one whit for her and seek only her dowry. No doubt you have pulled her into this scheme without her full awareness of what she is doing and why."

Lord Falconer's silence and the turning away of his head was answer enough to that particular question, and Henry closed his eyes again, rubbing one hand over his forehead as he thought about what he was to do next. Lady

Judith would have to be told, of course, and he could not hold any blame over her head now, not since he had learned the truth from Lord Falconer. She had been as much deceived as he had been.

"She was the one who tried to steal the ring from my hand, was she not?"

Finally, Lord Falconer looked back at him.

"She tried. She was not your partner but when you *did* have to step out to her during the course of the dance, she attempted to twist it from your finger. As I have said, it came about very quickly. I saw the ring on your finger and then spoke quickly to Lady Judith. She and I realized what we could do with such a seal and thus, she promised to try to steal it from you during the dance. I was disappointed in her failure, however – so much so that she said she would try again and promised to do it the second time."

Henry closed his eyes again, trying to keep control of his temper, which was threatening to explode from him. The manipulation, the deceit, and the sheer selfishness that Lord Falconer was displaying in his explanation was more than Henry felt he could bear. How had he never seen this in Lord Falconer before? They were friends, were they not? And yet this was a side of his character which Henry had never once seen, before this moment.

"She and I had practiced the action beforehand, of course, but it was not as successful as she had hoped. Again, she failed and, unfortunately, you were then convinced by Miss Bosworth that someone *was* attempting to steal the ring from you, which I was a little frustrated about – though I did end up agreeing and encouraging you to keep it back at your townhouse."

"No doubt in the hope that you might steal it from me more easily there."

Lord Falconer shrugged.

"It was only because you displayed it so easily the first night of our meeting this Season. Had you not done so, then I might have found someone else to take some money from. It is your own fault for showing that ring off!"

Henry could hardly believe what Lord Falconer was saying. It was as if everything he had said, everything he was attempting to explain was merely a deflection, a putting away of responsibility so that he did not feel any guilt whatsoever.

It was difficult to take it in.

"And now, no doubt, you have come to tell me that you knew I had attempted to take the ring from your neck this evening."

Henry shook his head.

"No, it was not you. Again, you used Lady Judith, did you not?"

His friend chuckled.

"I may have done. She is so very willing. It seems as if she is quite in love with me and therefore, will do anything that I ask of her."

Henry's stomach twisted.

"When she fell into me this evening, that was her opportunity."

"And it is not paste jewelry which she has in her possession," Lord Falconer finished, his eyes narrowing. "It is the real talisman ring."

Seeing no need to pretend, Henry nodded.

"Yes, she has the real one. I have no paste."

"So you lied to me."

A hard, callous laugh broke from Henry's lips.

"I hardly think that you are in the position to protest! How many lies have you said to me? How many deceitful words were spoken from your lips? I do not think that you have any right to be offended."

Lord Falconer narrowed his eyes all the more until they were nothing but slits.

"Get out of my way."

"If you think you are going to go back to her and claim the ring as your own, then you are quite mistaken." Henry stepped to one side, though his hands were still in fists. "But very well, go. See if you can find your lady – but be aware that I will speak to her myself, just as soon as I can, and tell her all that you have told me."

"I care not." Lord Falconer barged past Henry, one elbow jabbing out towards him as Henry stumbled back, fighting back the fire in his veins that told him to throw a punch back. "I will find another young lady with an even better dowry and–"

"Do not think that I will stay quiet on this." Gesturing for the footmen to go after Lord Falconer, they were forced to pause when the gentleman stopped dead, turning around to glare at Henry.

"What do you mean?"

"I am not about to stand silently by and permit everything you have done – or attempted to do – remain between us."

Lord Falconer scowled, his eyes growing dark.

"You are going to tell the very society you claim is much too condemnatory, much too disapproving, that I have done something you consider wrong?"

"That *I* consider?" Coming closer, Henry forced his feet to stand still, afraid now that he would suddenly launch himself at his supposed friend if he came any closer. "It is one thing to state that a lady defending her honor and that of her sisters simply by speaking her mind is unworthy of being pushed aside by society but quite another to claim that stealing and deceit is not anything worthy of note. The two are opposite." Flinging one arm out towards his study, he shook his head. "Not only that, but you also came into my home and injured my butler in your search for something of mine that you wanted for yourself. Believe me, it is for society's good that I will tell them about what you have done, and what sort of character you have. That way, I can assure you, other young ladies – such as Lady Judith – will be protected from you and your dark intentions. So go, Falconer. Go in the knowledge that you have not only failed in your attempts to steal from me, but also in your desire to keep such actions a secret. All will be revealed and there is nothing you can say or do which will protect you."

Silence fell and for some minutes, Henry wondered what it was that Lord Falconer was going to do. The man's shoulders were lifted, his eyes narrowed, and his face had gone a shade of purple as fury spread into every part of his expression. Henry stood resolute, refusing to be cowed as Lord Falconer took a step forward – and then the footmen moved and stood directly in his path.

"It is time for you to take your leave, Falconer. I assume it is clear enough already, but if it is not, let me state plainly that you are not welcome to set foot in my house – or upon my estate – again." Flexing his fingers, Henry let out his breath slowly, beginning to regain control of himself completely. "This is the last time I hope to ever speak with you, Lord Falconer. Now leave and do not come near me, or Miss Bosworth, again."

Lord Falconer let out a loud exclamation, made to start forward but the footmen once more were in his path. With dull eyes, Henry watched him being encouraged from the room and, once the door had closed behind him, fell back onto the couch and closed his eyes as a myriad of emotions swamped him.

Regret, embarrassment, and pain were the three foremost of his feelings and Henry let each one come to take its place. He had never expected his friend to be the one stealing from him, but it seemed that there was more to Lord Falconer and his friendship than there had appeared.

But it is over now.

Closing his eyes, Henry let his mind go to Miss Bosworth. He had left her at the ball, left her with Lady Judith and, whether or not she had been successful in gaining the truth from her, Henry could not guess. The desire to see her, the need to be close to her, swept through him and, before he could give himself even another moment to think, Henry found himself striding towards the door, a new energy rushing through him.

Amid all the pain and all the confusion, the only person he wished to see was Miss Bosworth. She would bring him all the comfort he needed.

EPILOGUE

"*Y*ou have something which does not belong to you."

Lady Judith blinked furiously, her face flushing pink.

"I beg your pardon?"

"You have an item from Lord Yarmouth in your possession," Joy said plainly, tilting her head a little. "You need not deny it, I know that Lord Falconer is courting you and that he is the one who has encouraged you to steal this ring from Lord Yarmouth. However, what is not at all clear is why *you* are so willing to engage in such behavior, especially given how much it will damage your reputation once it is made known."

"I – I beg your pardon?" The color faded from Lady Judith's face. "What do you mean by that?"

Joy lifted her eyebrows.

"I only mean that Lord Yarmouth has, at this very moment, gone to speak to Lord Falconer about what he has been trying to do. Once that conversation is at an end, he will declare to the *ton* what he has learned. That will include his connection to you, I am sure, and perhaps that *you* were the one who stole the ring from Lord Yarmouth."

A shiver ran over Lady Judith's frame, her eyes widening still more.

"You – you mean to say that society will know of it all?"

This was a lot easier than Joy had expected, for she had anticipated that Lady Judith would be more difficult to speak with than this.

"Yes." Joy shrugged. "I do not think that it is something which can be kept hidden." Lady Judith snatched in a breath, one hand at her mouth as she stared at Joy, turning to look at Miss Fairley thereafter who also nodded. Tears began to flood her eyes, but Joy remained resolute, refusing to give in to any sort of sympathy. What Lady Judith had done was wrong, and that ring ought to be returned just as soon as it could be, regardless of what Lady Judith herself felt. "Give it to me at once."

Speaking calmly but decisively, Joy held out one hand, and much to her surprise, Lady Judith simply pulled the ring and silver chain from her reticule and handed it to her directly. Joy slipped it into her reticule and tied the strings tightly.

"I – I am sorry." Lady Judith grasped Joy's hand tightly, her eyes now swimming with tears. "Lord Falconer told me that it was the only way for us to marry! He said that I had to steal the ring from Lord Yarmouth so that he could make certain that our marriage would be secured! Thus far our attachment has all been quite secretive, and I want to marry him more than anything else in this world."

Joy's heart twisted and Miss Fairley put out one hand to Lady Judith.

"Lord Falconer ought not to be doing anything of the

sort," she said, quietly. "I do not understand all of what has taken place, but it must have weighed on your conscience."

Lady Judith closed her eyes.

"My father insists that I have a gentleman of particular standing as my husband. Lord Falconer did not quite meet that standard, but he insisted that there was a way. He has told me that he loves me and–"

"I do not believe him, and neither should you." Joy closed her eyes in frustration over her own quick tongue as Lady Judith's face went pale and a tear slid down her cheek. "Forgive me, Lady Judith but I must speak truthfully. If Lord Falconer truly loved you, then he would not have demanded that you do such things as this."

Lady Judith closed her eyes and sniffed.

"If my reputation is tarnished, then I... I... I shall never marry. Perhaps I have made a dreadful mistake."

Miss Fairley's eyes turned to Joy's and the sympathy within them was within Joy's heart also.

"I will do my very best to make sure that your name is kept from this."

When Lady Judith's eyes flared, only for her expression to crumple, Joy's heart ached all the more. This was no act, she was sure of it. Lady Judith appeared completely broken by all that had taken place, and realizing now that Lord Falconer did not care for her in the way that she had believed must be all the more distressing.

"Come." Miss Fairley put one arm around Lady Judith's shoulders. "Let us go and sit over here."

Joy watched as Miss Fairley let a sobbing Lady Judith away, her heart growing heavier by the moment – only for a hand to touch her shoulder.

"Lady Judith is upset, I see."

The urge to throw herself into Lord Yarmouth's arms

was so strong, Joy could barely hold herself back. The gentleman smiled at her, a fire in his eyes which she had never seen before. A fire that she too felt within her own soul.

"Might you wish to step out with me for a few minutes?" His hand went to hers and Joy nodded fervently. "I will not keep you long, for fear of what society might think."

"Society thinks me still a wallflower," Joy replied, linking her arm through his. "I doubt they will even notice me."

Lord Yarmouth laughed.

"Mayhap on this occasion, I shall be grateful for your standing as a wallflower, if it means that I can take you from here without anyone being aware of it!"

Leading her through the door of the ballroom, he turned this way and that before stepping into what appeared to be a small parlor which, thankfully, was well lit.

Joy did not hesitate, unable to hold herself back from him for another moment. Leaning forward, she wrapped her arms around his neck and smiled softly when his arms encircled her waist. A long sigh escaped from him, and she felt the same relief wash through her.

"I have your ring."

"Do you?" Lord Yarmouth leaned back and Joy smiled, putting one hand to her reticule to find the ring and setting the other on his shoulder. "Lady Judith was rather eager to give it to me though..." Frowning, she shook her head. "I should like it if you would be careful to keep her name from the *ton,* with respect to all of this. No doubt you will be telling society what Lord Falconer has done, but given how distressed Lady Judith is, I believe that, while what she did was wrong, she did it because of his insistence – and because she was afraid of being parted from the gentleman she loved."

Lord Yarmouth took the ring from her but continued to hold her gaze, his eyebrows lifting.

"He told her that he loved her?"

"He did."

Closing his eyes, Lord Yarmouth's jaw jutted forward.

"He truly is a scoundrel."

Briefly, he told her everything that had taken place in the townhouse, and Joy listened with growing astonishment. Putting her hand to his cheek – and a little astonished by her own boldness – she smiled softly up at him.

"That must have been very difficult for you to hear – and to see. He was your friend."

"He deceived me, just as he deceived Lady Judith. I confess that the shock will take a little time to recover from, but I am glad to have learned the truth, at least." Smiling, he leaned into her hand. "And I am grateful for you."

"Oh?"

Her heart began to quicken as Lord Yarmouth turned his head and pressed a kiss to her palm.

"More grateful than I can express," he murmured, making her suddenly very aware of just how closely he held her. "Your wise thinking, your boldness, and your courage have made me admire everything about you. Your beauty leaves me breathless, and my only regret is not pursuing you sooner."

Joy could barely breathe, such was the passion and the wondrousness of his words. Suddenly, the talisman ring did not seem as important as it once had. The only thing she could give any attention to was Lord Yarmouth.

"I wanted to court you, but already, it has become more than that. I want to marry you, Joy." As if he were a little afraid of expressing such passions to her so soon after their courting had begun, Lord Yarmouth lowered his head and pulled his gaze with him. "It may be too soon but–"

"Yes." His head lifted just as quickly as it had dropped and he stared into Joy's eyes, a little uncomprehending. "Yes, I will marry you." Joy spoke quickly, but let her heart speak openly, expressing itself to him without hesitation. "I think you the most wonderful, respectable, and honorable gentleman in all of London. My heart quickens whenever I see you. My spirits soar whenever we are in company together. Why would I turn from that when I could have more than I have ever had before?"

Lord Yarmouth's smile came slowly, but his hands pulled her closer to him and, after a moment, he dropped his head again and this time, kissed her softly. It was the first time Joy had ever been kissed by a gentleman, but it was so astonishing, so wonderful and passionate, that even when he lifted his head, she kept her eyes closed simply to savor the moment a little longer.

"Might I give you this?"

When she opened her eyes, Lord Yarmouth was holding out the talisman ring, smiling at her.

"The ring? Your father's ring?"

He nodded.

"I have always wanted to give it to the lady I was to marry, to the lady I was to love and cherish for the rest of my days." Reaching for her hand, he caught it on his own and then pushed the ring onto her finger. "And I do love you, Joy."

She laughed quietly as the ring slipped from her finger almost the moment he took his hand away, given it was much too big.

"Perhaps I shall keep it on the chain for the moment, Lord Yarmouth? After all, we do not want to lose it again."

He grinned at her and then quickly slipped the ring onto the chain before leaning forward and clasping it around her neck. His fingers brushed at her neck and Joy shivered lightly, her smile growing as she felt the weight of the ring around her neck.

"Thank you," she whispered, putting her arms around his neck again as he willingly pulled her close. "You have brought me more joy than I ever imagined could be mine and yes, my dear Yarmouth, I love you too."

OH MY, that ring finally brought them together! I hope you enjoyed Joy and Lord Yarmouth's story.

WHILE WAITING for the next wallflower story, check out one of my earlier books, More Than a Companion Read ahead for a sneak peek!

MY DEAR READER

Thank you for reading and supporting my books! I hope this story brought you some escape from the real world into the always captivating Regency world. A good story, especially one with a happy ending, just brightens your day and makes you feel good! If you enjoyed the book, would you leave a review on Amazon? Reviews are always appreciated.

Below is a complete list of all my books! Why not click and see if one of them can keep you entertained for a few hours?

The Duke's Daughters Series
The Duke's Daughters: A Sweet Regency Romance Boxset
A Rogue for a Lady
My Restless Earl
Rescued by an Earl
In the Arms of an Earl
The Reluctant Marquess (Prequel)

A Smithfield Market Regency Romance
The Smithfield Market Romances: A Sweet Regency
Romance Boxset
The Rogue's Flower
Saved by the Scoundrel
Mending the Duke
The Baron's Malady

The Returned Lords of Grosvenor Square
The Returned Lords of Grosvenor Square: A Regency
Romance Boxset
The Waiting Bride
The Long Return
The Duke's Saving Grace
A New Home for the Duke

The Spinsters Guild
The Spinsters Guild: A Sweet Regency Romance Boxset
A New Beginning
The Disgraced Bride
A Gentleman's Revenge
A Foolish Wager
A Lord Undone

Convenient Arrangements
Convenient Arrangements: A Regency Romance
Collection
A Broken Betrothal
In Search of Love
Wed in Disgrace
Betrayal and Lies
A Past to Forget
Engaged to a Friend

Landon House
Landon House: A Regency Romance Boxset
Mistaken for a Rake
A Selfish Heart
A Love Unbroken
A Christmas Match
A Most Suitable Bride

An Expectation of Love

Second Chance Regency Romance
Second Chance Regency Romance Boxset
Loving the Scarred Soldier
Second Chance for Love
A Family of her Own
A Spinster No More

Soldiers and Sweethearts
To Trust a Viscount
Whispers of the Heart
Dare to Love a Marquess
Healing the Earl
A Lady's Brave Heart

Ladies on their Own: Governesses and Companions
Ladies on their Own Boxset
More Than a Companion
The Hidden Governess
The Companion and the Earl
More than a Governess
Protected by the Companion

Lost Fortunes, Found Love
A Viscount's Stolen Fortune
For Richer, For Poorer
Her Heart's Choice
A Dreadful Secret
Their Forgotten Love
His Convenient Match

Only for Love

The Heart of a Gentleman
A Lord or a Liar
The Earl's Unspoken Love
The Viscount's Unlikely Ally
The Highwayman's Hidden Heart
Miss Millington's Unexpected Suitor

Christmas Stories
The Uncatchable Earl
Love and Christmas Wishes: Three Regency Romance
Novellas
A Family for Christmas
Mistletoe Magic: A Regency Romance
Heart, Homes & Holidays: A Sweet Romance Anthology

Christmas Kisses Series
Christmas Kisses Box Set
The Lady's Christmas Kiss
The Viscount's Christmas Queen
Her Christmas Duke

Happy Reading!
All my love,
Rose

A SNEAK PEEK OF MORE
THAN A COMPANION

"*D*id you hear me, Honora?"

Miss Honora Gregory lifted her head at once, knowing that her father did not refer to her as 'Honora' very often and that he only did so when he was either irritated or angry with her.

"I do apologize, father, I was lost in my book," Honora replied, choosing to be truthful with her father rather than make excuses, despite the ire she feared would now follow. "Forgive my lack of consideration."

This seemed to soften Lord Greene just a little, for his scowl faded and his lips were no longer taut.

"I shall only repeat myself the once," her father said firmly, although there was no longer that hint of frustration in his voice. "There is very little money, Nora. I cannot give you a Season."

All thought of her book fled from Honora's mind as her eyes fixed to her father's, her chest suddenly tight. She had known that her father was struggling financially, although she had never been permitted to be aware of the details. But not to have a Season was deeply upsetting, and Honora had to immediately fight back hot tears which sprang into her eyes. There had always been a little hope in her heart, had always been a flicker of expectation that, despite knowing her father's situation, he might still be able to take her to London."

"Your aunt, however, is eager to go to London," Lord Greene continued, as Honora pressed one hand to her stomach in an attempt to soothe the sudden rolling and writhing which had captured her. He waved a hand dismissively, his expression twisting. "I do not know the reasons for it, given that she is widowed and, despite that, happily settled, but it seems she is determined to have some time in London this summer. Therefore, whilst you are not to have a Season of your own – you will not be presented or the like – you will go with your aunt to London."

Honora swallowed against the tightness in her throat, her hands twisting at her gown as she fought against a myriad of emotions.

"I am to be her companion?" she said, her voice only just a whisper as her father nodded.

She had always been aware that Lady Langdon, her aunt, had only ever considered her own happiness and her own situation, but to invite your niece to London as your companion rather than chaperone her for a Season surely spoke of selfishness!

"It is not what you might have hoped for, I know," her father continued, sounding resigned as a small sigh escaped his lips, his shoulders slumping. Honora looked up at him, seeing him now a little grey and realizing the full extent of his weariness. Some of her upset faded as she took in her father's demeanor, knowing that his lack of financial security was not his doing. The estate lands had done poorly these last three years, what with drought one year and flooding the next. As such, money had been ploughed into the ground to restore it and yet it would not become profitable again for at least another year. She could not blame her father for that. And yet, her heart had struggled against such news, trying to be glad that she would be in London but broken-hearted to learn that her aunt wanted her as her companion and nothing more. "I will not join you, of course," Lord Greene continued, coming a little closer to Honora and tilting his head just a fraction, studying his daughter carefully and, perhaps, all too aware of her inner turmoil. "You can, of course, choose to refuse your aunt's invitation – but I can offer you nothing more than what is being given to you at present, Nora. This may be your only opportunity to be in London."

Honora blinked rapidly against the sudden flow of hot tears that threatened to pour from her eyes, should she permit them.

"It is very good of my aunt," she managed to say, trying to be both gracious and thankful whilst ignoring the other, more negative feelings which troubled her. "Of course, I shall go."

Lord Greene smiled sadly, then reached out and settled one hand on Honora's shoulder, bending down just a little as he did so.

"My dear girl, would that I could give you more. You already have enough to endure, with the loss of your mother when you were just a child yourself. And now you have a poor father who cannot provide for you as he ought."

"I understand, Father," Honora replied quickly, not wanting to have her father's soul laden with guilt. "Pray, do not concern yourself. I shall be contented enough with what Lady Langdon has offered me."

Her father closed his eyes and let out another long sigh, accompanied this time with a shake of his head.

"She may be willing to allow you a little freedom, my dear girl," he said, without even the faintest trace of hope in his voice. "My sister has always been inclined to think only of herself, but there may yet be a change in her character."

Honora was still trying to accept the news that she was to be a companion to her aunt and could not make even a murmur of agreement. She closed her eyes, seeing a vision of herself standing in a ballroom, surrounded by ladies and gentlemen of the *ton*. She could almost hear the music, could almost feel the warmth on her skin... and then realized that she would be sitting quietly at the back of the room, able only to watch, and not to engage with any of it. Pain etched itself across her heart and Honora let out a long, slow breath, allowing the news to sink into her very soul.

"Thank you, Father." Her voice was hoarse but her words heartfelt, knowing that her father was doing his very best for her in the circumstances. "I will be a good companion for my aunt."

"I am sure that you will be, my dear," he said, quietly. "And I will pray that, despite everything, you might find a match – even in the difficulties that face us."

The smile faded from Honora's lips as, with that, her father left the room. There was very little chance of such a thing happening, as she was to be a companion rather than a debutante. The realization that she would be an afterthought, a lady worth nothing more than a mere glance from the moment that she set foot in London, began to tear away at Honora's heart, making her brow furrow and her lips pull downwards. There could be no moments of sheer enjoyment for her, no time when she was not considering all that was required of her as her aunt's companion. She would have to make certain that her thoughts were always fixed on her responsibilities, that her intentions were settled on her aunt at all times. Yes, there would be gentlemen to smile at and, on the rare chance, mayhap even converse with, but her aunt would not often permit such a thing, she was sure. Lady Langdon had her own reasons for going to London for the Season, whatever they were, and Honora was certain she would take every moment for herself.

"I must be grateful," Honora murmured to herself, setting aside her book completely as she rose from her chair and meandered towards the window.

Looking out at the grounds below, she took in the gardens, the pond to her right and the rose garden to her left. There were so many things here that held such beauty and, with it, such fond memories that there was a part of her, Honora had to admit, which did not want to leave it, did not want to set foot in London where she might find herself in a new and lower situation. There was security here, a comfort which encouraged her to remain, which told her to hold fast to all that she knew – but Honora was all too aware that she could not. Her future was not here. When her father passed away, if she was not wed, then Honora knew that she would be left to continue on as a companion, just to make certain that she had a home and enough coin for her later years. That was not the future she wanted but, she considered, it might very well be all that she could gain. Tears began to swell in her eyes, and she dropped her head, squeezing her eyes closed and forcing the tears back. This was the only opportunity she would have to go to London and, whilst it was not what she had hoped for, Honora had to accept it for what it was and begin to prepare herself for leaving her father's house – possibly, she considered, for good. Clasping both hands together, Honora drew in a long breath and let it out slowly as her eyes closed and her shoulders dropped.

A new part of her life was beginning. A new and unexpected future was being offered to her, and Honora had no other choice but to grasp it with both hands.

CHAPTER ONE

*P*ushing all doubt aside, Robert walked into White's with the air of someone who expected not only to be noticed, but to be greeted and exclaimed over in the most exaggerated manner. His chin lifted as he snapped his fingers towards one of the waiting footmen, giving him his request for the finest of brandies in short, sharp words. Then, he continued to make his way inside, his hands swinging loosely by his sides, his shoulders pulled back and his chest a little puffed out.

"Goodness, is that you?"

Robert grinned, his expectations seeming to be met, as a gentleman to his left rose to his feet and came towards him, only for him to stop suddenly and shake his head.

"Forgive me, you are not Lord Johnstone," he said, holding up both hands, palms out, towards Robert. "I thought that you were he, for you have a very similar appearance."

Grimacing, Robert shrugged and said not a word, making his way past the gentleman and finding a slight heat rising into his face. To be mistaken for another was one thing, but to remain entirely unrecognized was quite another! His doubts attempted to come rushing back. Surely someone would remember him, would remember what he had done last Season?

"Lord Crampton, good evening."

Much to his relief, Robert heard his title being spoken and turned his head to the right, seeing a gentleman sitting in a high-backed chair, a glass of brandy in his hand and a small smile on his face as he looked up at Robert.

"Good evening, Lord Marchmont," Robert replied, glad indeed that someone, at least, had recognized him. "I am back in London, as you can see."

"I hope you find it a pleasant visit," came the reply, only for Lord Marchmont to turn away and continue speaking to another gentleman sitting opposite – a man whom Robert had neither seen, nor was acquainted with. There was no suggestion from Lord Marchmont about introducing Robert to him and, irritated, Robert turned sharply away. His head dropped, his shoulders rounded, and he did not even attempt to keep his frustration out of his expression. His jaw tightened, his eyes blazed and his hands balled into fists.

Had they all forgotten him so quickly?

Practically flinging himself into a large, overstuffed armchair in the corner of White's, Robert began to mutter darkly to himself, almost angry about how he had been treated. Last Season he had been the talk of London! Why should he be so easily forgotten now? Unpleasant memories rose, of being inconspicuous, and disregarded, when he had first inherited his title. He attempted to push them aside, but his upset grew steadily so that even the brandy he was given by the footman – who had spent some minutes trying to find Lord Crampton – tasted like ash in his mouth. Nothing took his upset away and Robert wrapped it around his shoulders like a blanket, huddling against it and keeping it close to him.

He had not expected this. He had hoped to be not only remembered but celebrated! When he stepped into a room, he thought that he should be noticed. He *wanted* his name to be murmured by others, for it to be spread around the room that he had arrived! Instead, he was left with an almost painful frustration that he had been so quickly forgotten by the *ton* who, only a few months ago, had been his adoring admirers.

"Another brandy might help remove that look from your face." Robert did not so much as blink, hearing the man's voice but barely acknowledging it. "You are upset, I can tell." The man rose and came to sit opposite Robert, who finally was forced to recognize him. "That is no way for a gentleman to appear upon his first few days in London!"

Robert's lip curled. He should not, he knew, express his frustration so openly, but he found that he could not help himself.

"Good evening, Lord Burnley," he muttered, finding the man's broad smile and bright eyes to be nothing more than an irritation. "Are *you* enjoying the London Season thus far?"

Lord Burnley chuckled, his eyes dancing - which added to Robert's irritation all the more. He wanted to turn his head away, to make it plain to Lord Burnley that he did not enjoy his company and wanted very much to be free of it, but his standing as a gentleman would not permit him to do so.

"I have only been here a sennight but yes, I have found

a great deal of enjoyment thus far," Lord Burnley told him. "But you should expect that, should you not? After all, a gentleman coming to London for the Season comes for good company, fine wine, excellent conversation and to be in the company of beautiful young ladies – one of whom might even catch his eye!"

This was, of course, suggestive of the fact that Lord Burnley might have had his head turned already by one of the young women making their come out, but Robert was in no mood to enter such a discussion. Instead, he merely sighed, picked up his glass again and held it out to the nearby footman, who came over to them at once.

"Another," he grunted, as the man took his glass from him. "And for Lord Burnley here."

Lord Burnley chuckled again, the sound grating on Robert's skin.

"I am quite contented with what I have at present, although I thank you for your consideration," he replied, making Robert's brow lift in surprise. What sort of gentleman turned down the opportunity to drink fine brandy? Half wishing that Lord Burnley would take his leave so that he might sit here in silence and roll around in his frustration, Robert settled back in his chair, his arms crossed over his chest and his gaze turned away from Lord Burnley in the vain hope that this would encourage the man to take his leave. He realized that he was behaving churlishly, yet somehow, he could not prevent it – he had hoped so much, and so far, nothing was as he had expected. "So, you are returned to London," Lord Burnley said, making Robert roll his eyes at the ridiculous observation which, for whatever reason, Lord Burnley either did not notice or chose to ignore. "Do you have any particular intentions for this Season?"

Sending a lazy glance towards Lord Burnley, Robert shrugged.

"If you mean to ask whether or not I intend to pursue one particular young lady with the thought of matrimony in mind, then I must tell you that you are mistaken to even *think* that I should care for such a thing," he stated, plainly. "I am here only to enjoy myself."

"I see."

Lord Burnley gave no comment in judgment of Robert's statement, but Robert felt it nonetheless, quite certain that Lord Burnley now thought less of him for being here solely for his own endeavors. He scowled. Lord Burnley might have decided that it was the right time for him to wed, but Robert had no intention of doing so whatsoever. Given his good character, given his standing and his title, there would be very few young ladies who would suit him, and Robert knew that it would take a significant effort not only to first identify such a young lady but also to then make certain that she would suit him completely. It was not something that he wanted to put his energy into at present. For the moment, Robert had every intention of simply dancing and conversing and mayhap even calling upon the young ladies of the *ton,* but that would be for his own enjoyment rather than out of any real consideration.

Besides which, he told himself, *given that the* ton *will, no doubt, remember all that you did last Season, there will be many young ladies seeking out your company which would make it all the more difficult to choose only one, should you have any inclination to do so!*

"And are you to attend Lord Newport's ball tomorrow evening?"

Being pulled from his thoughts was an irritating inter-ruption and Robert let the long sigh fall from his lips without hesitation, sending it in Lord Burnley's direction who, much to Robert's frustration, did not even react to it.

"I am," Robert replied, grimacing. "Although I do hope that the other guests will not make too much of my arrival. I should not like to steal any attention away from Lord and Lady Newport."

Allowing himself a few moments of study, Robert looked back at Lord Burnley and waited to see if there was even a hint of awareness in his expression. Lord Burnley, however, merely shrugged one shoulder and turned his head away, making nothing at all of what Robert had told him. Gritting his teeth, Robert closed his eyes and tried to force out another long, calming breath. He did not need Lord Burnley to remember what he had done, nor to celebrate it. What was important was that the ladies of the *ton* recalled it, for then he would be more than certain to have their attention for the remainder of the Season – and that was precisely what Robert wanted. Their attention would elevate him in the eyes of the *ton*, would bring him into sharp relief against the other gentlemen who were enjoying the Season in London. He did not care what the gentlemen thought of him, he reminded himself, for their considerations were of no importance save for the fact that they might be able to invite him to various social occasions.

Robert's shoulders dropped and he opened his eyes. Coming to White's this evening had been a mistake. He ought to have made his way to some soiree or other, for he had many invitations already but, given that he had only arrived in London the day before, had thought it too early to make his entrance into society. That had been a mistake. The *ton* ought to know of his arrival just as soon as was possible, so that his name might begin to be whispered amongst them. He could not bear the idea that the pleasant notoriety he had experienced last Season might have faded already!

A small smile pulled at his lips as he considered this, his heart settling into a steady rhythm, free from frustration and upset now. Surely, it was not that he was not remembered by society, but rather that he had chosen the wrong place to make his entrance. The gentlemen of London would not make his return to society of any importance, given that they would be jealous and envious of his desirability in the eyes of the ladies of the *ton*, and therefore, he ought not to have expected such a thing from them! A quiet chuckle escaped his lips as Robert shook his head, passing one hand over his eyes for a moment. It had been a simple mistake and that mistake had brought him irritation and confusion – but that would soon be rectified, once he made his way into full London society.

"You appear to be in better spirits now, Lord Crampton."

Robert's brow lifted as he looked back at Lord Burnley, who was studying him with mild interest.

"I have just come to a realization," he answered, not wanting to go into a detailed explanation but at the same time, wanting to answer Lord Burnley's question. "I had hoped that I might have been greeted a little more warmly but, given my history, I realize now that I ought not to have expected it from a group of gentlemen."

Lord Burnley frowned.

"Your history?"

Robert's jaw tightened, wondering if it was truly that Lord Burnley did not know of what he spoke, or if he was saying such a thing simply to be a little irritating.

"You do not know?" he asked, his own brows drawing low over his eyes as he studied Lord Burnley's open expression. The man shook his head, his head tipping gently to one side in a questioning manner. "I am surprised. It was the talk of London!"

"Then I am certain you will be keen to inform me of it," Lord Burnley replied, his tone neither dull nor excited, making Robert's brow furrow all the more. "Was it something of significance?"

Robert gritted his teeth, finding it hard to believe that Lord Burnley, clearly present at last year's Season, did not know of what he spoke. For a moment, he thought he would not inform the fellow about it, given that he did not appear to be truly interested in what they spoke of, but then his pride won out and he began to explain.

"Are you acquainted with Lady Charlotte Fortescue?" he asked, seeing Lord Burnley shake his head. "She is the daughter of the Duke of Strathaven. Last Season, when I had only just stepped into the title of the Earl of Crampton, I discovered her being pulled away through Lord Kingsley's gardens by a most uncouth gentleman and, of course, in coming to her rescue, I struck the fellow a blow that had him knocked unconscious." His chin lifted slightly as he recalled that moment, remembering how Lady Charlotte had practically collapsed into his arms in the moments after he had struck the despicable Viscount Forthside and knocked him to the ground. Her father, the Duke of Strathaven, had been in search of his daughter and had found them both only a few minutes later, quickly followed by the Duchess of Strathaven. In fact, a small group of gentlemen and ladies had appeared in the gardens and had applauded him for his rescue – and news of it had quickly spread through London society. The Duke of Strathaven had been effusive in his appreciation and thankfulness for Robert's actions and Robert had reveled in it, finding that his newfound status within the *ton* was something to be enjoyed. He had assumed that it would continue into this Season and had told himself that, once he was at a ball or soiree with the ladies of the *ton*, his exaltation would continue. "The Duke and Duchess were, of course, very grateful," he finished, as Lord Burnley nodded slowly, although there was no exclamation of surprise on his lips nor a gasp of astonishment. "The gentlemen of London are likely a little envious of me, of course, but that is to be expected."

Much to his astonishment, Lord Burnley broke out into laughter at this statement, his eyes crinkling and his hand lifting his still-full glass towards Robert.

"Indeed, I am certain they are," he replied, his words filled with a sarcasm that could not be missed. "Good evening, Lord Crampton. I shall go now and tell the other gentlemen here in White's precisely who you are and what you have done. No doubt they shall come to speak to you at once, given your great and esteemed situation."

Robert set his jaw, his eyes a little narrowed as he watched Lord Burnley step away, all too aware of the man's cynicism. *It does not matter,* he told himself, firmly. *Lord Burnley, too, will be a little jealous of your success, and your standing in the* ton. *What else should you expect other than sarcasm and rebuttal?*

Rising to his feet, Robert set his shoulders and, with his head held high, made his way from White's, trying to ignore the niggle of doubt that entered his mind. Tomorrow, he told himself, he would find things much more improved. He would go to whatever occasion he wished and would find himself, of course, just as he had been last Season – practically revered by all those around him.

He could hardly wait.

WELL, he thinks very highly of himself, doesn't he? Check out the rest of the story in the Kindle store, More Than a Companion

JOIN MY MAILING LIST

Sign up for my newsletter to stay up to date on new releases, contests, giveaways, freebies, and deals!

Free book with signup!

Monthly Facebook Giveaways! Books and Amazon gift cards!
Join me on Facebook: https://www.
facebook.com/rosepearsonauthor

Website: www.RosePearsonAuthor.com

Follow me on Goodreads: Author Page

Printed in Great Britain
by Amazon

38195913R00126